BLOOD OF THE TRUE BELIEVER

BLOOD OF THE TRUE BELIEVER
BY BRANDANN R. HILL-MANN
BOOK II OF THE HOLE IN THE WORLD

Nicole,
  Thank you again!
Happy Reading!
  B.R. Hill-Mann

atmosphere press

Copyright © 2020 Brandann R. Hill-Mann

Published by Atmosphere Press

Cover design by Dominique Wesson
dominiquewessonartblog.tumblr.com

No part of this book may be reproduced
except in brief quotations and in reviews
without permission from the publisher.

10 9 8 7 6 5 4 3 2 1

Blood of the True Believer
2020, Brandann R. Hill-Mann

atmospherepress.com

For my Papa. I wish you could be here to see this.

Patrick J. Hascall 1933-2020

CHAPTER ONE

Innes

The text Innes received after trying to phone Kahrin three times wasn't the most reassuring. It simply read 'wait one.' That was it. No explanation. Innes pulled over to the next rest area and parked. One, in Kahrin minutes, had turned into almost fifteen when his phone buzzed in the cup holder.

"What's wrong?"

"Nothing's wrong." Innes laughed softly. It hadn't been long since they spoke last. Kahrin called him earlier that day to ask if he thought a little black bandage dress was too slutty for a first date. "Why are you whispering?"

A pause. Long enough that he thought she'd hung up.

"So no one hears me."

Oh, of course.

"Aren't you on your date?"

"Yeah. About that."

A toilet flushed.

"Are you peeing?" His laugh fell somewhere between incredulous and exasperated.

"Well, not anymore. I needed to excuse myself so I could call you back." As if that was the most obvious explanation. "Can you pick me up?"

"Sure." That made his plans for the night much easier.

"When?"

"Now." He heard a shuffling, and Kahrin let out a quiet grunt. "There's an employee parking lot behind *Le Mer*."

"Fancy. And way out of town. What about your date?" He grinned even though she couldn't see him.

"Can you pick me up or not?" A creak. The sound of something clattering.

She wasn't telling him the whole story, which wasn't unusual on its own. Not when it came to their respective dating lives, but this was weird, even for her.

"Kahrin, what are you doing?"

"How long?" A very loud crash, meaning she'd definitely dropped her phone. And she'd argued with him about the size of the protective case! He heard her scramble to pick it back up.

"It's cold."

"Are you climbing out a window? In a tight dress?"

"Don't worry, I'm not wearing nylons. Just hurry, okay?"

Sure. The nylons were the important piece of information here.

When he pulled into the employee lot at *Le Mer,* she was standing near a dumpster, beneath a small window, hopping back and forth in her bare feet, heels in one hand. Because who climbed out bathroom windows in heels? He looked at said window, and if she'd been anything other than petite, she may not have fit. It took her a moment to recognize his little car, and she waved as she skipped over, barely waiting until he'd fully stopped before pulling on the handle.

She groaned as she flopped into the passenger seat and slid an arm under her hair to keep from sitting on it. Even her brown skin could not hide the flush in her cheeks from the wind.

"Thank you so much, Pretty Mouth." She leaned across the seat and pecked a kiss against his cheek. She put her seatbelt on before dropping her shoes on the floor of the car and tucking her feet underneath her.

"Hi!" She grinned, showing her eyeteeth, slightly mismatched eyes sparkling as she watched him drive. "Did I know you were coming home?"

He shook his head. "Last-minute decision. I have the weekend off, nothing due Monday. I thought I'd come rescue my best friend from the certain peril of a nice night in a restaurant that would cost me a week's wages." His eyes slid to her before he looked back on the road. "Am I going to get an explanation?"

"I was bored." Hardly unusual for his best friend with her seemingly endless energy. "I think he bathes in his cologne, and he only drinks," her voice pitched to a low drawl, mimicking whom Innes could only presume was the mysterious date, "whisky. Single malt. One ice cube, please. It brings out the moss." Returning to her regular Kahrin voice, she added, "I think he was surprised that I don't drink."

"The scandal!" Which begged the question, "Where did you meet this guy?"

"Running." He lifted an eyebrow. That wasn't so weird, but he also didn't think that was the whole story. "I was crossing Main, and he ran the light and almost hit me."

"What?" He glanced at her. This was a new weird, even for her.

"I'm fine." Clearly. Not that getting nearly hit by a car would slow her down at all. In fact, history showed that a car accident still required a team of medical professionals to keep her still.

She chattered on, and his grin turned crooked at the familiar feeling of driving and listening to her do just that. "He was on the phone with like, China or something. I don't know. He tried to explain it tonight at dinner, but I stopped paying attention after appetizers. Anyway, he felt so bad about almost hitting me he offered to take me out."

"Uh-huh." He glanced at her again. "And?"

"And?"

Oh, come on now. She wasn't going to play stupid, was she? It took all his strength not to roll his eyes. "You know." 'Boring' seldom told him much. Their friend Carbry had become boring after a few dates but, to Innes' knowledge, she'd never bailed out a bathroom window while on a date with him. Carbry likely never took her to *Le Mer* either, but mostly because it didn't seem like her kind of place. Another piece to the puzzle. "What's wrong with this one?"

"Nothing's wrong, per se." She shrugged, and reached over to the backseat with one hand, returning with his sweatshirt. "I just got sick of hearing about his grandkids."

Innes did his best not to groan. This time he rolled his eyes so hard he feared they'd stick. "Grandkids?" he asked, feeling proud that he'd managed the restraint to not raise his voice in surprise.

"It's not that bad." She waved her hand like they were talking about halitosis she'd suffered through. "He's only, like, forty or fifty something, and started young."

What was he supposed to say to that? He nodded, keeping his promise not to judge as she 'explored her type,' which seemed to be a gamut of men ranging in various degrees of inappropriateness. After what happened with

BLOOD OF THE TRUE BELIEVER

Evan Greves, though, he'd promised to let her make her own decisions on people.

"Where's your coat?" It was warm for this time of year, but still just above freezing.

"I didn't want to carry one. And I've never been with an old guy."

"Old? Old enough to be your father, maybe."

"I wanted to see what the fuss was about."

"How very Sophia Loren of you."

She wiggled her head at him, sticking her tongue out and rolling her eyes. "Whatever. He should know a twenty-year-old is going to be a little immature. It can't be the first time he's been walked out on." She laughed, clearly not upset about it at all, which prompted his own laughter.

Hers was definitely a face he needed to see. He backed off of his interrogation. There was just one more question to ask. "Are you hungry?"

"Starving. I'd love something I can pronounce." She plucked at his sweatshirt. "If you think I'm dressed appropriately."

"You're not underdressed for diner chili fries." She made a sound of pleasure he only heard in very specific situations. Oh, yes, he did know all of her weaknesses. Then a thought occurred to him. "Where's the car?" Their car. He didn't need it anymore and had given it to her for her birthday, but she still called it theirs.

"Oh! I snuck it into the pay lot in town. He picked me up at the cafe." She must have noticed his expression because she lifted her hands defensively. "I wasn't going to let some old potential creep pick me up at my house."

"Of course not. That would be weird." He could picture Ma Quirke's aneurysm now.

"I know, right?" She wiggled in the seat to look at him, her face softer. "I missed you."

His face softened to match. "I missed you, too."

"So," she stretched the syllable out into several, "what in the Private Life of Pretty Mouth has brought you to seek my wise counsel?"

That was a conversation he was hoping to avoid until later. Now that she'd brought it up, he'd only be able to dodge her for so long. "Do you have room for a malt, too?"

CHAPTER TWO

Kahrin

Chili cheese fries tasted better when your best friend shared them with you. This was an objective fact, tested and verified countless times over many years. There was also hardly a topic not bettered with the presence of a chocolate milkshake and two straws.

Kahrin didn't want to talk about her date. His name was David, of all things. How pedestrian. A curiosity had piqued when the man got out of his car to apologize and got a little too personal for her comfort, and now she'd explored that discomfort and decided it wasn't the kind for her. Serendipity was Innes showing up in town when she needed an extraction plan.

It was almost like magic, except she couldn't see or touch or be affected by magic, being a Hole in the World.

Innes didn't probe too much. Thank God. He seemed content that she'd decided David wasn't a type who held her interest. At least not totally.

"I don't know," she told him with a shrug, dragging one of the fat diner fries through a swirled glob of chili and that weird vinyl cheese that made all things better. "The fancy dinner was kind of neat."

"You said you didn't like the food," Innes reminded her. Holding one straw of their shake between his thumb and forefinger, he bobbed it up and down, folding the whipped cream into the rest.

"Yes," she agreed, because yes, she'd said that, "but I kind of like the part about being fussed over, and there was a lot of that."

She stuffed the fry in her mouth, decided she was full, and pulled her arms inside the orange sweater she'd stolen, nay, borrowed, nay, liberated from his back seat. Innes gasped theatrically at this brand-new information, which wasn't new at all, prompting her to roll her eyes.

"We'll call this a win in the name of science."

"Oh, you're into science now?" He reached out, and even though Kahrin knew what was about to happen, she failed to get out of the way in time to dodge the dollop of whipped cream that now adorned her nose.

She wrinkled her nose, making a huge deal out of the inconvenience until he surrendered, leaning in to kiss the cream away. "I will have you know that I am officially a college student. A student of the sciences, even."

The waitress came by and left the check on the table, knowing them long enough to tell when they'd lost steam and when not to interrupt a conversation. "So you told me. Every few minutes, by text, updating me on the process of applying." He held up his phone as she swiped up the check—a clever distraction in her opinion—and switched through several messages, including photos of each of her textbooks. "And the riveting adventures in the bookstore."

"Fine. Mock me." She dug into her purse, counting up the cash needed, figuring the tip, and setting the pile of it under the condiment caddy.

"Never. Well, not about this." Her eyes met his, big, bistre in contrast to his pale skin, and full of affection. "I'm proud of you."

She looked down at her lap, pulling at the stretchy fabric of her dress, a warmth spreading over her face. So many people pushed her to go to college, but Innes supported her when she wasn't sure, all the while reminding her that she could, even if she didn't want to. "It's not medical school." She lifted and dropped her thin shoulders. "Just sports medicine. Bandages and ice packs."

"Hey," he crooked a finger under her chin and tipped her face up so she couldn't avoid his gaze. She didn't try, smiling shyly at that eponymous mouth and squared jaw she knew from memory. His greying hair, less and less brown every time she saw him, artfully styled to look not styled. His carefully trimmed facial hair, with the little patch that didn't grow anymore, which was apparently what happened when you were kissed by a unicorn. "Whatever you choose to do, I'm proud of you because you're doing it. As long as you're happy."

She tipped her head side to side, as if shaking off the grin fighting to show itself. There were times in her life where his approval meant everything, and this was definitely one of them. "I am. I'm learning so much! And, my Anatomy professor says I'm *promising*."

"You can tell me all about it in the car." He nudged her, knowing too well the right places to poke and prod to make her squeal and hop out of the booth should she have any notions of resisting. Not all of the other patrons appreciated it, but one of the few charms of being in such a small town was that almost everyone knew them well enough to keep their thoughts to themselves.

She wore her shoes long enough to get to the parking lot, then hopped up on Innes' back to be carried the rest of the way. Heels really were the worst, but she did like how they made her rear look. What was the point of having such a nice figure if she couldn't flaunt it? Though, if she were honest, she wouldn't complain if she had a little more chest.

"Is Brodie expecting you?" She knew the answer before she asked, only needing the slight shake of his head to confirm his elder brother did not know he was in town. She rested her chin on his shoulder. "So...does that mean you need a place to stay?"

"If I might be so bold as to impose." Impose. Ma would have birthed literal kittens if she found out he'd come home and not stayed with them.

She grinned, pleased. "Well, with Brecken and Alec both gone, we have the space." As if he was going to sleep all alone on one of their old bunk beds.

Innes unceremoniously dumped her in the passenger seat. She leaned back, enjoying the easy way they fell into rhythm as if he'd never left. Even when he didn't get the chance to come back for months at a time, and she couldn't find the time to drive up to see him, every visit felt like picking up from the day before. She chattered away as he turned onto the dirt road leading out of town, giving him the abridged version of her latest string of jobs—another thing he never judged her for—and slightly more interesting stories about her classes.

"Look who's a nerd, now!" she said.

His mouth pulled to the side in thought. "Your professor has you call him André?"

"Yeah. We're all adults, he says." A fair point, in her opinion, and it made it easier to talk to him. "He's really funny. He wears bowties. Did you know people still wear those? With suspenders. And his arms are so long he has to roll up his sleeves to the elbows, but it works for him."

"That seems really familiar for a college professor."

What did that mean?

She shrugged. "I think it's nice."

"That's all that matters, then." He didn't say anything else until they arrived at the farm, where he pulled into his usual spot by the goat pen. Even the snow couldn't hide the ruts in the ground from all the times he'd parked and backed out of there.

His hands tapped on the steering wheel, and he didn't turn the car off right away. Even if she hadn't known him since they were still bedwetters, she'd have known something was on his mind. She turned sideways in her seat, legs folded beneath her. "What's going on, Pretty Mouth? We've talked about me all night. Even I can't pretend that I'm that interesting."

He sighed, letting his head fall back against the headrest. "I think I met someone."

Oh? Well, that had her undivided attention. "You *think* you met someone? What? Did you run into her and forget to get her name?"

"No." He chuckled. "I know her name. Evangeline. That's not what I mean." Kahrin didn't interrupt and tipped her head to lean against the seat. "I mean, she's nice and lives in my building. Sometimes we stand in the hallway and chat, and we've gone to lunch a time or two." Oof. Lunch dates. He really was giving this Evangeline the arm's length treatment. "I think she wants...more."

"More?" She still wasn't seeing the problem. "Is more bad? I thought you wanted more." The difference between them: he dreamed of more with someone, like in the storybooks he loved so much, and she was content to flit from one thing to the next.

"I do." He looked at her and shrugged. "She wants exclusivity. I don't know if I'm ready for that. You know, I have to stay focused on my studies." Nerd. "And there are...things I'm not ready to give up."

Kahrin frowned, going on the offensive, a protective surge rising in her. "She's not pushing you into anything, right?"

"No. No, it's nothing like that." He huffed, and Kahrin saw lights turn on in the kitchen as Ma came out to see who was in the driveway. "You know what? It's not a big deal." She did not believe that for a fraction of a second. "We should go inside before your Ma comes out with a ladle or something."

She shot him a look, lifting one of her brows.

"I want to spend time with my best friend. I can worry about Evangeline later."

Kahrin nodded, skeptical, as she slid her shoes back on. "Okay. But this is a pause, not a stop on the conversation."

"Do I have to carry you inside, too?"

She pouted out her lower lip, giving him her best helpless maiden expression. She was far from it, and he knew that, but it was part of their dance. "My shoes are new, and my feet hurt."

CHAPTER THREE

Kahrin

Judging by the reactions of her parents, Kahrin might have thought she brought the Pope home. Ma was already bustling around the house before they left the mudroom. She groused about being caught unaware though she remained cheery and fussed over Innes anyhow. "You terrible boy! I don't even have a pie made, and I don't think Kahrin's washed the sheets on the trundle in weeks."

Da was standing in the corner of the dining room, arms crossed, when they lugged Innes' bag in. His face remained stoic, making the tattoos that bisected his eye more severe. "We have spare beds now," he pointed out, his eyes seeking Innes'. Innes blanched under his stare.

"Da, stop it," Kahrin chastised affectionately at the same time her mother did.

"Nonsense," Ma clucked. "Those are Alec and Brecken's beds. What if they come home?"

Da snorted, though it was not a derisive sound. In Kahrin's opinion, his disliking Innes act held a lot less weight after the night they'd freed Yelena. It was Innes he trusted not to leave Kahrin alone while she remained unconscious in the hospital after her undeniably stupid heroics. If anything, she would say he softened toward Innes, becoming as protective over her best friend as he was his only daughter.

"My date was fine, by the way," she announced to divert attention.

It didn't work. Kahrin heard her mother in the kitchen, scooting her stepstool across the floor, followed by a clatter of dishes. "Iskandar," she called, her voice in that sing-song lilt that wrapped Da around any finger she chose, "where's that nice mustard?"

"Ma," Kahrin hollered to the kitchen, putting a pin in the discussion of where Innes would or would not sleep, "we just ate." She looked at Innes and lifted her hands in a helpless gesture.

"I promise you, it's not the only meal I've eaten today, ma'am," Innes said. Kahrin giggled softly into his shoulder as she leaned against him.

Ma tutted. "Innes you're too thin!"

"And tired," Kahrin cut in. "Remember all the driving?"

The mention of driving drew Ma's attention, her notice never failing her. "Is that your car in the yard?" So close to escaping.

"Yes, ma'am." He shuffled from one foot to the other, forcing Kahrin to shift her weight to avoid falling over.

Mention of the new car drew Da's attention as well, and he moved from the dining area to the kitchen where he could see the goat pen. "Small. Good on gas?"

"Yes, sir. That was the reason for choosing it." Innes scuffed a socked toe against the floorboard, discomfort settling on his shoulders that Kahrin couldn't place.

Ma came out of the kitchen, a plate of ham sandwiches in one hand and shooting an accusatory glance Kahrin's way. "If I had known you were coming home, I would have made a roast." She set the plate near them on the table and waved her hand as if embarrassed to put so lowly an offering in front of them. "How are you affording that?" she asked casually as she sat on one of the long benches on either side of their table.

"Grainne," Da said, more warning in his voice than Kahrin had ever heard him use with Ma before. Kahrin fanned her hands to either side, her expression asking Ma what was wrong with her.

Innes cleared his throat. "I, uh, had a little help with the financing."

Wait, what? Now Kahrin turned her look upon Innes, a questioning brow shooting up.

"It's not a big deal," he explained to her in a low murmur. "Don't ask. It's not interesting at all."

Yes, because that was her reputation, just letting things go. Now her curiosity was piqued and would not be sated until she had a chance to prod him. She reached across the table, her toes barely skimming the floor as she grabbed the plate of sandwiches. "We have catching up to do. I promise you can stuff us full of eggs and potatoes in the morning." She almost said sausage, but she had other plans for that.

Kahrin hopped down from the table and grasped Innes' hand with her empty one, headed for the stairs. "Your adoring fans will need to wait until tomorrow," she teased.

Up they went, through Brecken and Alec's room, and into the little room she called her own. She could have moved out into the bigger one when her brothers moved out, but this tiny room—more of a storage alcove, really— was hers. It had a window, and her running medals were pinned to a memento board on her purple wall. There were silly candids stuck right next to photos from all the proms Innes accompanied her to. Her trundled daybed was not exactly something a grown woman would have. Probably. But it was hers. This room was hers, growth ticks marked on the wall, dent in the slanted ceiling from bouncing on her bed, and all.

She set the plate on the bureau and started the process of shedding her oppressive dress in favor of pajamas. Which, she was sure he'd notice, was also one of his shirts, pilfered when helping him move into the shoebox he called a room at his university.

"So," she started over her shoulder, "you had help with the financing. What does that mean, Pretty Mouth?" Freed from her dress, she tossed it aside and left it on the floor until she could be bothered to pick it up.

She might have guessed that it would bother Innes before her. He set his things down and crossed to pick the dress up. "I told you: it's not a big deal. I was wasting a lot of study time on the public bus—at least an hour each way—and a, um, friend helped me out."

"A friend?" He was dodging something, and if he was dodging it with her, there was a reason. Despite the way her curiosity screamed out, she let it go, for now, as she snatched the dress from his hand and stuffed it in the laundry basket. "Hey, if it helps you better use that big, beautiful—"

"Ruggedly handsome."

"Ruggedly handsome brain of yours," she finished with an exaggerated roll of her eyes, reaching to tousle his hair even as he dodged it, "then I'm all for it."

"You forgot the best part." She let a squeal as he grabbed her around the waist and pulled her close to him, immediately leading her into a waltz, of all things. Where did he learn to waltz? "It lets me come home more often."

Well, that mollified her, and put a genuine grin on her face. Enough that she clean forgot to interrogate him on his new dancing skills, and instead leaned into it, her feet finding the steps after only a few stumbles.

"Well, when you put it that way." Far be it from her to argue with something so obviously for her benefit. "Fine," she said, lying her head on his chest. "You'll share your secrets when you're ready, so I won't pick, on account of my growing as a person."

He chuckled, dropping a kiss to the top of her head before releasing her so he could retrieve his own sleep clothes. Bundled up in blankets against the winter chill, which was already frosting her window, Kahrin abandoned her bed to snuggle on the trundle. As was tradition. "Tell me about the girl, so I can pretend to be jealous."

He laughed, awkward again. "There's nothing to tell, really. I told you everything I know." Not exactly. There were lots of things to tell, like her last name and how much bigger her boobs probably were than Kahrin's. But, again, he dodged it. "Do you mind if we don't talk about her?" He ducked forward and stole a kiss, which was enough to refocus her attention. "Or anything?"

Well, it would be rude to decline such a generous invitation. She wiggled about until she seated herself upright in his lap, facing him. "That, my ruggedly handsome best friend, is my distraction tactic. I should tell you to get your own thing." But she wouldn't. She was only a woman, after all, and this was an ideal end to a night that started with a lousy date.

CHAPTER FOUR

Innes

It followed logic that if Innes wanted to spend the most time possible with Kahrin on his weekend home, he needed to join her in the things she did. Failure to think this through to a logical conclusion found him huffing and puffing, sweating and panting, and not in the fun way that had ensured his good night's sleep.

"How far has it been?" he asked as he sucked in an ice-cold breath and lengthened his stride to catch up. "It has to have been, I don't know, ten miles."

"Not yet two," she called over her shoulder. And then, because his best friend was a jerk, she turned about and jogged backward just in front of him.

"It feels like ten." Likely it would feel like more, later. He wasn't even out of shape!

She turned around again, slowing to run at his side. And how long would that last? He could see her practically vibrating to move faster. "Now you know why I said we'd eat after a run. What if your stomach was full of toast and eggs? Do you know how bad that tastes the second time?"

That was not helping. Not even a little. "You really do this every day?" It was a silly question, as he already knew the answer. He'd known the answer since they were twelve. "Every-every day?"

"No." Well, that made him feel better. "Sometimes I go twice." She had to be kidding. She dropped back again.

"Where are you going?" He didn't trust her behind him. Not when he was barely keeping up, and she seemed to gain wind with every stride.

"Well, I don't want to run off and leave you alone," the fact that she could carry on a conversation without dropping dead was unbelievable, "just in case you collapse." She picked up her pace, passing him, and *ran back around the other side again.* She was literally running circles around him! That was just unnecessary. "Besides, this way you can't escape me when I ask you more about Evangeline."

His mouth pulled into a tight line, though not for long, since it seemed the only possible way to keep breathing was through his mouth now that the cold had frozen his nose shut. "There's not much to tell." Obviously this was not true, since he'd already confessed to visiting so he could talk to Kahrin about it. "She's nice. She's pretty."

Kahrin jogged backward at his side, her ponytail bobbing with her exaggerated movements. "I figured that part out. What do you like—or not like—about her?"

Both were excellent questions. What did he like about her? It was difficult to remember anything specific about their encounters. "I don't want to be pushed into a commitment right now."

"Because of school." She didn't phrase it as such, but it was definitely a question.

"Not just school."

"Because of the droves of women flinging themselves at you on a daily basis?"

He snorted, since his lungs burned from the cold. While

not technically untrue, he was not ready to elaborate. How did he explain Emilia, and how she fit into, well, all of this?

"Or," his wily best friend started, her voice taking on a tone he knew well, "maybe it's all an excuse. Judging by the way you're huffing and puffing here." She fell behind him once more, making another circle so she could toss her taunt over her shoulder. "Maybe you're just not up to the challenge? Afraid you'll give small-town boys a bad rep if you buckle?"

That was the final straw. Waiting until she was dropping behind him once more, he lunged, not giving her a chance to dance out of his way as she could often do. He grabbed her up and slung her over his shoulder, shrieking for him to put her down. Which might have been more convincing if she hadn't been squealing with glee.

"I'm done running," he announced, skipping down off the road into the woods, not even sorry that his sneakers filled with snow that would soak his socks.

Being that this was not the first time he'd hefted her like a bag of feed, he knew enough to wrap an arm around her legs to avoid getting kicked in the head.

"Innes Cameron, you put me down!" she yelled out, laughing and beating her tiny fists against his backside. Had there been any sincerity in the act, or in her words, he'd have put her down right away. They both knew that.

"Are you sure that's what you want?" he asked, loosening his grip just enough to give the impression he'd drop her into the snow. She screamed, her laughter taking on a frantic quality as her demands turned to pleading not to drop her. So, he did what any mature university man would do: he dropped into the snow, cushioning her fall as he took her with him. The bank, deeper than he'd anticipated, covered them both, causing Kahrin to holler out as the snow crept under her collar and into the gap between her sweater and running tights.

It didn't take her long to squirm around until she could straddle him, her fingers finding the spots in his ribs she knew would make him buck and laugh, turning the tables, or at least the snowdrift, against him. He fought back, grasping her wrists and yanking her closer to stop her vicious attack. He leaned up to nip at her throat, harder than he'd done other times, and pinned her wrists behind her as his pulse thundered in his ears. He felt her tense and drew back to see her face. She looked at him, her eyes widening nearly imperceptibly, but enough that he let go without hesitation.

She hopped up and skittered back, breathless and laughing, but giving him an uncertain look. "What're you doing, Pretty Mouth?"

He felt his stomach drop. "Kahrin, I'm sorry." He pushed up from the ground, ignoring the bite of snow against his skin, mad at himself. "I shouldn't have done that. I mean, not without asking."

She looked at him, a brow raised as her breathing settled. "Asking what?" Yes, what? That was a good question. Of course, he knew the answer. In the moment, it just felt like a natural thing to do. "To restrain me?"

"No," he said as he held his hands up. Though, she wasn't wrong. "I mean, yes. I know I should have asked first. You know I wouldn't—"

"I didn't say I didn't like it." Wait, what? "It's just...new. And not really like you."

No, it wasn't. Was it? "Kahrin, I'm really sorry."

She shook her head, not looking any less confused, but

something dancing in her mismatched hazel eyes all the same. "Are you?" Of course he was! How could she even ask that? She waved a hand to stop him from protesting. "I mean, is that something you...want to do? To me?"

Innes could feel his face heat, and he fumbled for words, tearing a hand through his hair. "I..." He'd not expected that feeling in his stomach. The spark of warmth at the idea. A not so gentle nudge to see where the thought lead. Kahrin didn't know how not like him this was, but he wasn't ready for her to ask questions. Mostly because he wasn't sure how to explain it, yet. "I mean..."

She lifted and dropped her shoulders as she brushed some snow off her hair. Her eyes locked on his as her hands absently rubbed at opposite wrists in alternating twists. "So, ask." Wait, *what*? She gnawed at her lip in a way he found very distracting, presenting a few ideas he hadn't expected to have. "Or don't." She took a deep breath and held it, her pulse thrumming visibly under the red mark at her throat, which spiked his own. He'd not thought of it, not until it was right there in front of him. "You know I trust you."

Well, that was enough, wasn't it? He let a low, growling laugh, feeling a little out of his element, and yet... She twitched back half a step as he strode toward her. Prowled. She didn't move farther than that. Her eyes seemed uncertain, but her lips twitched at the corners and she stood her ground as if to challenge him. He swept her backward, pushing her until her back hit a silver maple, one of her wrists in each of his hands. "Are you sure?"

She laughed this time, breaking some of the tension, something for which he was grateful. "Yes, now stop asking. I know what to say if that changes."

He blinked. Of course she did. Because it had always been an agreement between them. Long before they'd ever, as she liked to put it, ruined her maidenhood. *Vigil*. A nod back to the days when they would sit watch on the porch of the farmhouse, waiting for something to appear. A faery. A monster they'd only seen in their dreams. Proof of the magic he knew existed, long before they met Yelena, and long before either of them knew that Kahrin couldn't experience magic.

Still, he asked. Just to be sure. "Promise?"

She nodded, and just in case that wasn't enough, tugged at her arms until he let her lift them above her head. "I promise." She laughed softly, the sound sending an unexpected tingle through him that he felt far below his belly. He found himself wondering why he'd never considered this, with Kahrin, until just now. Considering the new education and exploration that came with Emilia's friendship, he had to wonder if this added ache to experience it with his best friend was one more bullet on the list of the reasons to not date Evangeline. "Besides, you're not going to have sex with me out here, in the middle of the woods. Not with people and potential unicorns wandering about."

She was right. Even though she wasn't as funny as she thought she was, he laughed. Because, well, she was as funny as she thought she was. He gripped her wrists more firmly, watching, listening for any signs she was in distress. The delicate thrum of her pulse rushed against his grip as he ducked his head and demanded a kiss from her. He followed the flutter of it over her neck to where it joined her ear, at which point he faltered into a chuckle. If you couldn't explore new things with a friend, then what was the point? And Kahrin wasn't just his friend. She was the oldest, dearest friend he had.

Kahrin was right about him. He valued privacy too much, so they didn't do it right then and there against the tree. But, that didn't mean there was nothing of note. Snatched gasps. Teasing touches. Scraping of teeth over pulse points. The chill of ice and snow against hot skin. An exploration of something slightly darker, something to follow up on later. If she was willing.

The thrill of something new buzzed between them. Through breakfast. While cleaning up after their extensive cardio workout. While he was driving back to school at the end of the weekend. He'd accomplished the exact opposite of what he had intended for his visit. He'd come home to not have to think, and left with a great deal on his mind.

CHAPTER FIVE

Kahrin

Kahrin had an unexpected number of things on her mind as she watched Innes drive away on Monday morning. Things which tumbled around in her head through breakfast and during the drive to the community college. Things that made it difficult to focus during her first lecture.

Given their closeness and the friendship they'd built over years, it surprised no one when Kahrin and Innes had shifted into a physical relationship without the entanglements of romantic love. They didn't need it. What they had worked for them, and even more so after Innes left for university. It reassured them both that anything that remained between them was an active choice, not one of obligation. That they would eventually take those physical explorations in other directions seemed natural, as well. So why did she feel odd? Uncomfortable in a way that felt both right and wrong at once? And where had that instinct in her best friend been hiding?

"Miss Quirke?" Kahrin looked up, only just realizing that she'd puzzled away the entire period of Anatomy. André watched her with intense brown eyes as the other students filed out, in a hurry to reach their jobs or next classes. "Are you all right?"

"Oh!" She looked down at her notes, which had turned into doodles which looked vaguely like trees in snow. She paused, desperate for something clever to say. "Yes." That was not it. "Why would you ask?"

André waited until the last student was gone before answering. "You seem distracted today."

Something about the way he pitched his voice made her look around the room, as if she worried someone might hear the honeyed tones it dropped into.

"I didn't sleep much." She waved a hand and smiled as she stood to gather up her things, shoving her textbook and notebook into her bag. "I'm sorry. Don't worry, I'll—"

André stopped her with a lift of a hand, leaning his weight on the other. "You don't owe me an explanation. I'm just concerned." He smiled, and she noticed it wasn't exactly the type of smile a teacher should direct at a student, and she looked around the room once more, the end of her long braid winding around her hand.

"It's nothing. Really." She slung her bag over one shoulder and untucked her light scarf from under it, realigning it to conceal anything that might or might not have been lingering just out of her shirt collar. Oops. "Have a good day," she said, passing his desk to leave.

"Miss Quirke? Kahrin?"

Kahrin paused at the door, turning around to look at him again. He was still smiling at her, and she lifted her eyebrow, feeling her cheeks pink at the sound of her name from a very generous mouth. There was no denying he was nice to look at, his jaw angular and all the lines of his face sharp. Something tingled through her, knowing the way he was looking at her, like he could unhinge his jaw and swallow her whole, shouldn't excite her. And, yet?

"Is there something you need, professor?" And now she sounded like she was in a bad porno. Wonderful.

He gestured at the overhead projector, and then to the pages in front of him. "Would you like to look at my lecture notes?" He must have sensed she her confusion from the way she blinked at him several times. "Since you were so dazed? I wouldn't want you to get behind because something," he canted his head, "or someone was distracting you."

She ducked her head, her mouth betraying her with a wide grin. Now she spun the end of her braid in front of her. "I wouldn't want to hold you up. It's my own fault."

"I'm going to get coffee." He lifted and shook his empty travel mug. "I have a break between classes." He tilted his head toward the window, indicating the town outside. "I usually go to the cafe to prep."

What did that have to do with...*Oh*. She checked over her shoulder again. Was she looking for eavesdroppers? Jokesters? A hidden camera to catch her being made a fool of? Or worse? She turned up a grin and tried to appear less on the back foot. "Are you offering to help me study, or asking me on a date?" Bold? Yes. But so was his invitation, and the consequences if she guessed wrong. She needed him to be clear.

André stood, leaning against the wall in that sort of pose men did to look casual when they were trying to be cool. "That depends."

"On?"

"How badly your answer bruises my ego." He flashed a smile at her, the kind that said he was used to the fact that he was cute getting him through things that others wouldn't have managed. Everything about him said as much, from his pink bowtie which had no right looking good on him, to the buttoned shirt tucked into his jeans. Jeans. Who wore a bowtie with *jeans*?

She laughed, feeling heat creep up her neck. "Is that allowed? You're my teacher." She didn't know a lot of things, and she had a knack for making foolish decisions—such as stabbing herself in the guts to save her best friend and a unicorn—but even she knew that teachers weren't supposed to date their students. Right?

André switched off the projector and closed the computer linked to it. He gathered up his papers and slid them into a manilla file folder. Kahrin watched him, fixed to the spot as he did so, like she was in one of those dreams where she was suddenly naked in front of everyone who ever hated her. There was no way this was real. Someone was punking her. They had to be.

He picked up the folder and walked—no, he strode—toward her and held it out. She noticed that there wasn't much space between them. No room for the Lord, as her Ma would say.

"Are you going to tell on me?" There was that smile again, bright as the sun through the windows and making her belly flip over.

She shook her head. Which she knew was the wrong answer. She could see Da staring in disapproval. She could hear Ma tutting. She could even hear Innes, in the back of her mind, asking her what she was thinking, and following it up with that characteristic "hm?" he used when making a point. The fact that she knew it was the wrong answer made it...more exciting?

André leaned down the good foot and more of height between them, his mouth near her ear as he tapped the folder into her hand. "I thought not."

She blinked, a frown turning her mouth down as she took the folder, pausing uncharacteristically to consider the options before her. He stood up straight and chucked her under the chin with a fist before returning to his table to gather his things. Her ear tickled, and the place where he'd touched her sang with sensation that stirred heat in her belly and downward. His eyes stayed on her as he slid into his puffy vest, one arm and then the next.

"You can get what you need from them here and then leave them on the projector." He slung his messenger bag across his chest and ran a hand through his curls. Her fingers twitched, imagining what they felt like. "Or, you can bring them to the cafe, and I can talk you through them."

"Talk me through them?" She lifted her brows, giving him a teasing rebuke. "Because I can't read? Half of this is pictures to label."

"You got me." He smiled, like he had a secret. One he was bursting to tell her if only she had the right activation code. "I just want to talk to you. Outside of class." Well, at least he knew this was a dodgy proposition. That had to mean something, right? "So, if you come by the cafe, coffee's on me. Shut the door when you leave. It locks itself."

And then he left.

Kahrin stared at the doorway. What just happened? She still wasn't sure, but she felt her lips stretch into a wide grin that almost hurt her face. She ducked her head, tucking a lock of hair behind her ear. She bounced on the balls of her feet, her tall boots creaking. She looked at the file folder, chewing her lip. What was she afraid of? This was new, and she liked new things. Wasn't she just pinned to a tree, enjoying the way the bark scraped her back when her shirt slid away from the waist of her running tights? If she hadn't been brave, that would never have happened. So now, was she going to be brave, or was she going to sit down and study quietly?

She'd never been good at quietly.

CHAPTER SIX

Innes

Innes saw the box leaning against the door to his top floor efficiency as he mounted the stairs. He shook his head, not sure what he expected. How he thought he could go out of town and not be missed. He had his keys in his hand before stooping down to pick it up. He jiggled the keys, finally getting the door open with a loud protest from the hinges. They needed replacing, as they weren't strong enough for the heavy door. Another thing he determined he would learn and do on his own.

He tossed his ruck to the floor just inside before examining the box. Right away he could tell it was clothing, though it had a little heft to it. More often than not it was clothing. No university student in his income bracket had any business owning the array of suits and tuxedos which hung in his small closet. He didn't actually know why he needed so many. Maybe he didn't. Maybe Emilia just enjoyed dressing him same as she delighted in touting him around on her arm. He wasn't going to refuse good tailoring. He had a great butt, and great butts belonged in great-fitting pants.

He realized as he lifted the lid of the box to peek inside, it wasn't just clothes. He wasn't sure what it was, some sort of metal...cage. The metal was polished, the curve of it sleek, and a very familiar length. Was he supposed to put his... in that? It didn't look exactly comfortable, and a not small (and similarly curved) part of him tingled with the thrill of something new. That was part of the excitement of this entire affair, and likely exactly the reaction Emilia intended from him. It explained his last set of measurements at his, ah, previous trouser fitting. He'd assumed she was just having a bit of fun. He'd not expected to be so correct. Wicked woman.

"Hi, Innes."

He hurriedly put the lid back in place, clearing his throat and hoping his face wasn't as red as it felt. He turned around to find Evangeline standing across the hall in her doorway. Tall and slender, she leaned against the doorframe, her shiny ginger hair piled in a knot on top of her head and looking like an extra from a movie about ballet. Pink sweater, hanging from one shoulder, leggings, and—this last part almost made him laugh out loud—leg warmers. He coughed to cover the laugh, trying to put the contents of the box out of his mind and think of something clever to say. "Hello."

Smooth.

"Missed you this weekend." She smiled at him over the brim of a mug. "I had to fold laundry all alone." Yet he spied a white plastic basket piled with dirty laundry tucked under one arm, and a steaming mug in the other hand.

He dipped his head forward and shook it with a grin. There was no denying she was pretty. Only someone not paying attention would miss that she liked him, with the way she was always *right there.* Not so much that it was disturbing, but she would rival Kahrin in tenacity. Innes had enough on his plate without adding her to it, no matter how flattering it was to have her attention. This weekend had cemented that in his mind. "Are you sure you managed?"

"I was lonely, not helpless." Her whisky-brown eyes crinkled at the corners. "And I didn't finish it all." She nodded at the basket propped against her hip. "Saved some for you. Where'd you go all weekend?" She shook her head, tittering, as if she could erase the words like an Etch-A-Sketch. "You don't have to answer that. I'm being too nosy."

He smiled. She made it easy to smile. "It's not a big secret. I went home." There wasn't much to tell beyond that, nothing that would interest her. "Spent some much-needed time with my best friend."

"He must have been glad to see you." She took a noisy sip from the mug.

"Um, she, actually." He could have sworn he'd told her that, but maybe he hadn't. Honestly, he'd been so busy between his studies and the other activities he'd committed to, he couldn't remember what he'd told her. "I've known her since forever."

This warranted no comment from Evangeline. "Are you going to offer to help me? I have my hands full out here."

What? "Oh, um. I have class soon, so I should clean up." He patted his stomach like he was in a children's pantomime. "I still have to eat." But...he was a gentleman, and she every bit the maiden fair. He leaned the box inside his door, then crossed the narrow hallway and took the basket under one long arm. "I can at least get you down the stairs."

"That's so sweet of you to offer!" Evangeline pushed her weight away from the door, her slightly uneven gait closing the already small space between them. "Boop!" She tapped the end of his nose with the tip of one finger, stiffly as if pressing an elevator signal, making him twitch it, but his smile brightened all the same. "The laundry can wait! I can cook while you shower. Do you like French toast?"

Innes shook his head to rid an odd haze that came over him, stutter-stepping backward toward his own door. What was so off-putting about the idea of letting a very pretty woman into his apartment? He pulled his door shut with his free hand and wrangled the keys out of it. "That's a really nice offer, but we don't want your laundry to get cold." What? Somehow, he could hear Kahrin laughing at him. "Um, rain check?"

"On breakfast? Or that dinner you promised to go to with me?" She tilted her head, that bubbling, effervescent giggle filling his ears once more. She was teasing him, and he found he didn't mind as she stepped closer. "You know, if we planned well, we could do one and wake up to the other."

He took a deep breath and prepped a gentle rebuff. She smelled like sugar. Just...sugar. Sweet and pure. That was not the scent of a terrifying woman. So, she was a close talker. It let her keep her voice lower, making sure her words traveled no further than his ears. It was cute when he thought about it.

"I can't. At least not tonight," he managed at last. His evening was, apparently, spoken for. "Let's get this downstairs, hm?"

Evangeline took a step back, looking abashed. "I'm being pushy."

"No! It's fine. Really. My best friend would say it's not your fault, that my good looks are a curse." He shrugged, relaxing into a *what can I do?* pose. "I'm just busy."

"Okay. I get it." Her expression fell, but she did her best to keep her smile in place as they started down the stairs. "Look, it's okay if you don't like me. You don't have to pretend just to spare my feelings."

"No, it's not that." His hand sprang up in front of him in placation. He really didn't enjoy disappointing her, as she was very nice to talk to, and to look at, and she did little—and not so little—things to let him know she was interested. But it was better for him to be honest than to lead her on, right?

He stopped at the first landing and met her eyes as her hitched step brought her down the stairs. "I do like you." After all, this was why he'd gone home. He'd meant to talk about this more with Kahrin. To ask if his priorities were wrong. If the fun he had at all these parties with Emilia, and all she was teaching him in return, were the wrong thing to choose right now? But then he'd surprised Kahrin, and himself, with what came during their run, and that added another layer to his thoughts. "It's not a good time for me."

Evangeline chewed on one full, pink lip, which he found very distracting, and surely not helping them...what were they doing? He couldn't remember.

"Okay." She tapped his chest with a finger as she stepped past him down the next turn of stairs. The place she touched felt singed beneath his shirt. "But you'll let me know the moment your schedule clears up?"

"You'll be the," he did a quick, exaggerated count on his fingers before hurrying behind her, "fourth to know. The other women in my life scare me." Heaven help him should they ever meet. "Maybe we can start with a drink?" His smile pulled wide as they took the remaining stairs side by side, and suddenly Innes couldn't remember what he was even protesting. He stopped when she reached the door to the basement laundry room, subconsciously leaning into the space between them. His phone buzzed in his pocket, snapping him back into his right mind. He slid the phone from his pocket just long enough to see the caller. Emilia. Impeccable timing. "I have to take this." He blinked several times, as if dazzled by sun on snow.

She reached with one hand, warmed from the mug, and brushed her thumb against the little bald patch along his jaw. He flinched away. He thought he caught a flash of a frown, but a flutter of his eyes later and it vanished. She was just a sweet smile again.

She accepted her basket from him. "I'm pushing again. Don't worry: I'll be more patient. I have a feeling you're worth waiting for."

"There's no right response I can give you." He waggled a finger at her, stepping backward up the stairs. It felt wrong for her to touch Yelena's kiss. Very wrong. His low chuckle masked his discomfort. "That's a trap. You're trying to trap me."

Evangeline set the basket on the beat-up metal table near the dual set of washers and dryers. She lifted a hand in a helpless gesture. "Innes, if I were trying to trap you, you'd be caught."

CHAPTER SEVEN

Kahrin

What was the point of dropping so much money on a cute little black dress if you weren't going to get mileage out of it? A denim jacket and trainers and boom! Kahrin had wrangled another outfit from it! She suspected she'd get many first date uses out of it. Of course, this would only be logistical so long as every date was a first date. And with her track record of flitting through people it seemed realistic, and she didn't see why André would be an exception.

Was this a first date? The donning of her now named First Date Dress suggested it, but they'd had such a nice time at the cafe. Surprising no one who knew her, if she chose to tell them, not a lot of studying or prep took place. Well, maybe prep for this date. Which she decided was the first. Hence, the First Date Dress.

Granted, the dress wasn't practical in this weather. But! She looked cute. As if that was hard to do when someone was so naturally blessed with good genetics as she was.

She waited by the corner at the cafe, her car tucked into the pay lot again. She'd not asked exactly how old André was, but she was pretty sure it was in the realm of over thirty, and she wasn't going to risk questions from Da. Not yet. If this was just a one-off, there was no need to endure a lecture. And if it wasn't? No. She wasn't ready to think about that. She wasn't even sure she wanted *more* as an option. Twenty was hardly time for settling down, and Kahrin quite liked the unknown parts of her life right now. At the moment, her romantic adventures still qualified.

She sent a quick text to Innes. A one-word text at any point in the night and he would call with some crisis or another to give her an excuse out of the date. She looked up as André pulled up in his car. His smartcar. A little coupe that made almost no sound as he veered toward the curb and stopped.

Before she could reach for the handle, André held up his hands and hopped out of the car, jogging around it—in jogging shoes no less—to open the door for her. He was considerably dressed down from the other day, especially compared to her and her First Date Dress. Suddenly even the denim jacket didn't feel like it was putting in enough effort to play down her outfit.

He pulled the door open and gestured for her to get in. "I should do this right, huh?"

Kahrin crossed her arms, stepped back, and looked him up and down, her expression half teasing, but also confused. "You're joking, right?"

It was his turn to look confused. "About what?"

"You're in a hoodie, with a smug little car, and you're opening the door like this is a fancy date?" She laughed, shaking her head.

He frowned. "What's so funny about my car?" He stepped back and crossed his arms. "Carbon emissions are a serious issue, Kahrin. We each need to be responsible for our footprint on the planet."

"I know." She drew the two syllables out. Of all the things she'd listed, she hadn't expected that to be the point of contention. She waved her hands in front of her, dismissing her words. "I didn't mean anything by it. I get the seven generations lecture from my Da, too." Since it seemed they were not discussing the dress code, she got into the passenger seat, smoothing her skirt beneath her as she swung her feet in. He closed the door and returned to his side. Even for her tiny frame, the car seemed compact. But it was fine, and she made a note not to make fun of his car again.

She'd agitated him, that much was clear. He said nothing as he got in the car and started driving. He didn't even turn the radio on, so she reached forward and did so, a classical program whining to life. He glanced at her, then back at the road. "Just ask next time."

She nodded, perplexed by the complete shift in his demeanor from the other day. The effusive and chatty man who had hunched over a cafe table in the corner with her, making her laugh so much that she needed twice as long to copy his notes, was apparently not in this car. Five minutes in and she'd ruined things, apparently.

"So," she hesitated, sucking at her teeth before going on, "where are we going? You were so mysterious about it."

That seemed to perk him up. His eyes danced again as he quickly glanced to her. She couldn't lie; she liked the way he looked at her. There was something overwhelming about it, like it could consume her, and not necessarily in a good way. "It's a surprise."

She smiled, though something made her uneasy. She looked out the window as he turned the car toward the main road out of town. "What kind of surprise?"

"There's a place a little way out of town," he explained. "Toward the country, before all the farms start." There was that smile again, the one that was too charming to get mad at, and he knew it. As if his whole life it had gotten him anything he wanted. "I thought we could have a picnic. You know, under the stars."

"In January?"

"No bugs." He reached over and squeezed her knee. She wasn't opposed to being touched, even less so by a very attractive man, but she jumped. "What's wrong?"

"I just want to know where we're going," she said, holding very still until he removed his hand. "That's all."

A line creased his brow and he let out a heavy sigh. "I told you where we're going. There's an empty field and—"

"Near the lot of quonsets?"

Grinning, he nodded. "That's right! You can see everything. The stars. The lights from the city. I can show you the different constellations you can see this time of year." He laughed. "It's kind of magical, if you believe in that nonsense."

"I don't think so." Her hands balled into fists without her meaning them to. "You know, I think this was a bad idea."

"What are you talking about?"

"Can you stop the car, André?" They hadn't reached the bridge over the creek yet. She could get back on foot to her car, no problem.

"Why?" He slowed but didn't stop. "Kahrin, what's wrong? You're being weird."

"I said stop the car!" She had her seatbelt off already and was grabbing at the handle. "I'm getting out whether you stop or not."

He pulled over. "You can't be serious? Where are you going?"

She was out of the car before it fully stopped. "You're taking me out of town? For a picnic in thirty-degree weather in the middle of the night?" She threw her hands up, her panic rising. And, yeah, maybe it was a little crazy, but she thought she could feel a burning in the scar up her stomach. "Did you think you were getting lucky?"

"Yeah, actually, though I would not be so crass about it." He ran a hand over his hair, ruffling the curls. "I don't know what I expected."

"Meaning?"

"I mean, I don't know why I thought someone your age had the maturity I was looking for." He waved a hand, beckoning her back into the car. "Let me drive you back to town."

Kahrin scoffed. "No."

"What do you mean, no? Are you going to walk all the way back?" He rolled his eyes. "Fine. You're hot, but that's not worth," he waved a hand around again, "whatever this is."

"Well, I can tell you what it is," she snapped back, her voice as icy as the side of the road. "It's a stupid, immature mistake to go out with your teacher." She slammed the door to the car and started walking away. She turned around and threw double birds at the back of his stupid smartcar as her eyes filled with tears.

She shouted, "And I'm dropping your shitty class."

CHAPTER EIGHT

Innes

Innes really needed to fix this door. He jiggled the keys, waiting for the barrel to turn over, and still had to lift up on the knob to get it to open. He was too tired for this right now. It would have to wait until he had time. Maybe over the weekend. Except the weekend started tomorrow, and he'd already promised out his time. The door would have to go to bed lonely, he supposed.

The inside of the apartment was dark. He needed to think about getting lights with timers, which Emilia insisted he do. If he was to continue stubbornly living in such an unsecure cinder block, as she put it, he needed to take minor security measures. He chuckled to himself with an undertone of affection, knowing that it was a matter of days before she sent someone to fix every little imperfection with his room, real or perceived in her *artiste's* mind. If he gave her keys, he was sure she'd try to redecorate out of her fondness for him. He knew it was her way.

He set his bag down and started tidying up. He left in a rush that morning, apparently scattering a stack of handwritten flashcards all over the floor without notice. He followed the trail of them to the table and set them next to the stack of books, open and piled in a semicircle around the only chair not covered with study materials. After a few minutes he'd done the few dishes that needed washed and put away his clean laundry. He slid out of his jeans, changing into sleep pants, and was just about to get into bed when a knock sounded on his door.

Because he wasn't a monster, he pulled the blankets back in place before he padded across the floor. Just before reaching the door, he noticed a hole in the toe of his sock and stooped down to pull them off hastily.

On the other side of the peephole, all smile and a cascade of strawberry-blonde hair artfully twisted over her shoulders, was Evangeline. She held a mug in each hand. The chain clacked as he opened the door just enough that he could stand in it. "Hi."

Her shoulders popped upward toward her ears. "You're home late." She tossed her head to shift a section of hair out of her eye. "Not that I was waiting for you." She jerked her chin to the side to indicate her apartment behind her. "I was reading and heard your keys in the door." She held up the mugs. "You said we could start with drinks. How about hot chocolate?"

"Oh." He rubbed at the back of his neck. "I was just about to go to bed. It's been a long day." When her face fell, despite her trying to hide it, he winced. What was he doing? Evangeline had been nothing but sweet to him, if somewhat earnest. He knew so many people who would give eyeteeth for such a thing. This was not how the hero would treat the maiden in any good story! He held a hand out for one of the mugs. "But staying up just a little longer probably won't hurt me." Who needed sleep, anyhow? Certainly no one in pre-med.

Evangeline's warm brown eyes lit up, as if he'd just made her whole day. Maybe he had. He honestly didn't know much about her life, and the little house made into their apartments was hardly exciting. Perhaps she was just lonely. He could understand that; sometimes he was, too.

She grinned when he opened the door further, finding himself wondering what it might take to get her to smile that way again. He stood back to let her past him, the pleasing scent of sweetness wafting past as she did. He closed the door.

"So this is your place?" She walked around the single room, her eyes taking in all 300 square feet in all its glory, while holding her mug in both hands. "It's nice."

"I'm sure yours is just as nice." Maybe even decorated with more than a cutaway human anatomy chart and a shelf of storybooks. There were four efficiencies on this floor, and he was pretty sure each one was laid out the same. Even so, there was nothing cruel in his voice, only some mild teasing.

"I've decorated a little more," she answered his unspoken question. She took a sip of her hot chocolate. "You should come see it sometime. It might give you ideas." Her sweater slid off her shoulder when she shrugged, giving him some ideas, for certain. "Like that one," she taunted, pointing her finger at him as if she could read his thoughts.

His face reddened. "I didn't mean to...I'm sorry. Like I said. Long day." He chuckled, abashed. "Sorry."

"Sorry for what?" She stepped across the floor, that little hitch in her gait barely notable. Maybe because his senses were dulled by studying before he came home. That uneven stride brought her a little closer than he was expecting. "I like you, Innes. I've been trying to get your attention since I moved in. You were so nice to help me, and I haven't stopped thinking of you since."

He laughed, running a hand over his hair. "Anyone would have done the same." Her height made it more difficult to avoid her eyes than to look into them. Molten and brown, making him feel as if he might be falling into them.

"Well, they didn't. You did." She tapped his mug, indicating he should take a sip, which he started to do when she again reached a finger to touch the missing patch of stubble on his jaw. He ducked away, setting his mug on the table.

"Did I do something wrong?" She tilted her head. "Does it hurt when I do that?"

"What? No." He covered it with his hand, protectively. "Nothing like that." He didn't want her touching it, which made no sense to him. Kahrin did, all the time, brushing it with a thumb in awe. That didn't bother him. So what was his aversion to letting Evangeline do so? It didn't feel right, but he couldn't pinpoint why.

She narrowed her eyes, her pretty pink lips twitching at the corners. "What is it? A childhood scar?" Her voice dropped to a playful whisper. "Did a unicorn kiss you?"

Wait, what? Was she teasing him? Of course she was teasing, she had to be and he did the same in return. "Yes, actually!" She couldn't possibly know the truth, but sometimes truth was more challenging to believe than a lie. "You guessed it." His smile turned lopsided, and he shrugged. He plucked up his courage, and this time he closed the distance, the diminishing space between them making his head rush. "But she left me."

"You poor thing. You must have been heartbroken." She was close enough now that he could smell bittersweet chocolate on her breath.

"It wasn't her fault, and I had good people around to help me through it."

"Your hot chocolate's getting cold." She stepped back to pick up the mug and hand it to him once more. He accepted it and lifted it to take a drink.

Before he could, he heard footsteps in the hallway, and before the door even opened, he knew who would be bursting through it. "Kahrin?"

"Pretty Mouth." Her voice cracked as she strode in, making herself at home as she dropped her keys and bag on the floor, pushed right past Evangeline, and slid her arms around his waist. Evangeline stepped back with a huff. He blinked, as if shaken awake, and curled himself around her, instinctively and protectively. Her tears always broke his heart. She was a mess. Cheeks stained with tracks of mascara. Did she even own a coat anymore? It was far too cold for just a light denim jacket, especially in that dress! "He's an asshole."

Well, asshole could apply to a good number of people, but it wouldn't do him any good to pry it out of her before she was ready. Instead, he dropped a kiss onto the crown of her head. "It's okay. You're here now." He didn't need to ask why. She never drove out here on her own without provocation, so he knew it must be important. "Here." He handed her his mug of hot chocolate. "Take a sip of this and breathe."

"Ah, that's not—" Evangeline stopped when she realized no one was paying attention to her anymore.

"Thank you." Kahrin accepted the mug and took a big drink, her nose wrinkling up instantly as she spat it back into the mug. "Ew. I think the milk is spoiled." She walked to the sink and dumped the rest of it down, rinsing it away. "You should throw yours out, too." She stopped mid-step on her way back across the room, as if only noticing Evangeline for the first time. "Who're you?" she demanded.

"This is my neighbor, Evangeline." He nodded toward the diminutive whirlwind of woman who'd swept into the apartment. "My best friend, Kahrin."

Kahrin's smile was tight as she inspected the woman, then softened as she held her hand out to shake. Evangeline reached for it, then pulled back at the last moment.

"I should get going."

Innes gave Evangeline an apologetic look. "I need to take care of this."

Evangeline tried to smile, though something lingered in her eyes as she took the pair of them in. "I'll talk to you later."

"Yeah, okay." Kahrin, unfazed by anything other than her immediate problem, waved to her back as she left, then looked at Innes. "I didn't mean to interrupt."

"You didn't," he said, shaking his head as some weird fog lifted. "Well, you did, but that's okay. You're here now. Go wash your face because you'll kill me if anyone else sees you like that, and I'll get you something to sleep in. Then, *soft shit* and talk, hm?" Curling up in a nest of blankets and chattering until they drifted to sleep would benefit more than just Kahrin.

There it was. The glimmer of amusement and that hint of smile as she tried to pretend *soft shit* wasn't exactly why she was here. "I guess. If you insist, I suppose it's the least I can do for barging in."

CHAPTER NINE

Kahrin

Something was wrong.

Kahrin wasn't sure how to put it into words, and it might have been easy to brush it away as jealousy—she was only human—but something about Evangeline seemed wrong. Almost hostile. Maybe it was Kahrin's reaction to her disgusting hot chocolate. Or, okay, maybe the way she'd burst into the room like she owned the place and instantly demanded all of Innes' attention. That might have put Kahrin off, had the roles been reversed. Even so, Evangeline looked at her like she was gum on the heel of a fancy shoe.

Maybe this was why they didn't meet their respective dates.

"I'm sorry," Kahrin began. Her face washed, Innes brought her a T-shirt and she changed into it without preamble. "She didn't have to leave; I intruded."

"You did," he said levelly, though his lips twitched. "But I don't mind. She's—"

"Intense?" She held up her hands to ward off his look of rebuke. "What? She is. When I walked in the door, she was looking at you like she wanted to—"

He wiggled his fingers like claws in front of him. "Like she wanted to kiss me? The horrors!" Kahrin rolled her eyes, her mood lifting. She squealed as he grabbed her up in his arms and growled into her neck. "Or what if she wanted to neck?"

"Who says that anymore?" she asked as she let him throw them both onto the bed. "Are you suddenly a grandpa?" She giggled as she bounced, and she noted how it was definitely not the old, lumpy mattress they'd helped him move in. Not that she was complaining that she wouldn't have a stiff back and bent neck in the morning.

"Did your hot date the other night ask you to neck? Or did he want to skip straight to the heavy petting?" He pulled her close to him and hugged her tight even as she poked her tongue at him. "Do you want to tell me why you're here?"

Well, that sucked the fun right out of the moment, didn't it? "We were talking about you," she reminded him. Because talking about the weird, intense girl who looked ready to spread jam on him was easier than picking through whatever she'd run away from. Besides, she was not ready for one of his famed (and inevitable) lectures just yet. "And the very pretty redhead I chased out."

"Do you think she's pretty?" Really? He was going to counter with that? Kahrin's eyes were going to roll out of her head at this rate. "I mean I could get her number for you, if you want."

"Shut up." She tangled her legs up with his and let out a sigh, prompting him to squeeze tighter until she wiggled and laughed to make him loosen his arms. "Fine. But you don't get out of talking about her forever. Since I assume that's the girl that sent you running to my arms last weekend?"

"Correct." He paused, and for a moment she really

thought he was going to relent and tell her the story. She was wrong. Sadly. "So. What happened?"

She grunted. She was dreading this part, even though she'd come here to tell him about it. She knew how he was going to react. So she tried to find the best, or at least most efficient way to deliver all of the information.

"I just had a bad date." Which wasn't unusual. Most of her dates sucked in some way or another. She'd bolted on one guy because he smelled too much like her Da, with some combination of corn husker's lotion and original Old Spice. "He wanted to go on a picnic or stargazing or something." She had to elaborate on that before she insulted Innes, since those were very much things they could and would do together. "Out by those quonsets." She bit down on her lip.

"Oh," he said, the word a few syllables longer than it required on a page. "Not really a happy place to be alone with a strange man."

"Something about getting stabbed—"

"Stabbing yourself."

"To save your life, if you recall," she reminded him. "And no one died."

"I was there. Yes," he reminded her right back. "But I also remember a few days when I wasn't so sure that would be the case." He kissed the crown of her head. Even now, three years later, vestiges of that near-miss still hung over them.

"I guess it just makes me jumpy." She turned her eyes up to see his, knowing this expression of her self-perceived weakness was safe with him. "And no one else understands." She brushed her hand with reverence over that place on his jaw, her brown fingertips tickling where

BLOOD OF THE TRUE BELIEVER

Yelena had nuzzled him in her true form. Smooth skin, just a smidgen pinker than the surrounding beige skin beneath his mostly brown stubble. "He yelled at me, and I was too upset to explain it."

"You shouldn't have to explain it," Innes reminded her. "When you express your needs, they should be listened to." Then, he frowned. At her or at something on his mind, she couldn't say, and decided not to pick at it. Just yet.

She'd been lucky, growing up with her best friend. He understood her, understood what she needed to hear, and understood how to support her. He was always the smarter of them with all his books and reading, but he got wiser every day. She hadn't known she needed to hear something like that until he said it.

"Thank you."

She didn't need much more from him after that, lying in the quiet, feeling safe in the safest place she knew. There was nothing she had to hide from Innes. He knew about Yelena. He knew the truth about what happened to Evan Greves. He knew she'd not been stabbed in a jealous rage by an inappropriately older man, which was the story they told others. And, he knew the strangest things about her, from the way magic did not affect her to the way her blood sang under the pressure of having her hands pinned above her head. That last one was new, even to her, but he knew it all the same.

"I just need to be loved right now," she told him quietly, turning her head to brush her nose against his jaw. "And be with someone I trust." She always knew what Innes wanted from her just as well as he knew what she wanted from him.

"Nothing could be simpler," he murmured before

drawing her into a kiss, sweet and gentle until she leaned up into it, with a soft hum of relief. She let him pull her atop him as he rolled to his back, his hands finding the fastest route to guide them together. It was familiar and easy, but never boring. Far from it.

In fact, what passed was a night of further exploration, as if simply picking up a conversation they'd left off back at the farmhouse. Kahrin Brigid Quirke was no stranger to sex, nor was her best friend, but Innes provoked something in her now. Something baser and bursting with sensations she'd considered but felt too ashamed ever to give voice to. His grip was painfully tight, on her wrists, on her hips, digging into the flesh of her rear. His movements were sharp and, at times, unrestrained. His voice dipped low into a gravelly tenor as he growled his wants against her skin. She gave all he asked, indulging in the new without fear, and finding the voice to make a few demands of her own. In fact, she pleaded, and found she quite liked the look it put in his eyes.

All of this with a good deal of laughter, of course. Because what was the point of sex with your best friend if you couldn't make it fun?

Less surprising was finding she liked the vestiges of aches in her muscles as she woke and slipped out of the bed before the sun was all the way up. She kissed the tip of Innes' nose as she pulled the covers back up around him. It took her a few minutes to find enough clothing to defend her against the falling snow and wind outside, and set out to see if she could find that little bakery she recalled passing on the way in the night before. She pulled the door closed behind her, using Innes' keys to secure it.

She made it two steps before she jumped, letting a bark

of surprise as she nearly walked into the chest of the woman from last night. She didn't, but only because the tall, thin, ginger woman stepped back with a very subtle limp, as if some unseen force pushed them apart. Her round, brown eyes stared down at Kahrin, and she crossed her willowy arms over her chest.

"Good morning," Kahrin chirruped. "Evangeline, right?" She thumbed over her shoulder toward the stairs down. "I was going out to find breakfast." Her lips pursed one way and then the other, and she shuffled her weight from foot to foot. "Would you like to come along?"

Evangeline's lips thinned, the blush pink draining from them. The corners twitched into something that was almost a smile, but not a happy one, and her thinly groomed eyebrows arched high.

"No. I don't think so." Terse. No explanation. No thanks. Now, Kahrin didn't have the best manners, but even she knew that was less than appropriate for teatime.

Kahrin just nodded. Something was not right. "Okay. Well, I'll see you around then." Kahrin stepped around the woman to start down the stairs.

"Will you be staying long?" she asked over her shoulder, not moving, eyes trained on Kahrin like one might watch a roach skitter across the floor into the dark space behind the stove.

"Maybe," she started, slowly. "We haven't talked about it." She jerked her thumb toward Innes' door. "He's not even awake yet."

"Oh." Evangeline's eyes narrowed and Kahrin could have sworn they flashed, from deep brown to bright gold, or bronze. It was hard to tell from where she stood. It could have been a trick of the light. It could have been Kahrin's sleep deprived imagination. She couldn't be sure.

Kahrin's mouth yanked up on one side as her brow furrowed. "Not to make this all trashy TV drama, but do you have a problem with me being here?"

Evangeline lifted her chin, her expression going cold like a witch's tit in a brass bra. "Should I?"

What did that mean? This conversation had spun into very odd territory very quickly. Warnings started going off inside her head, that odd feeling of off-ness moving swiftly to alarm. She crossed her arms, her own gaze cooling. "Maybe you should."

A puff of air came from Evangeline's nose. "You should be careful out there. It's bad weather for holes." Kahrin's eyes flickered wide. "You know, potholes. In the streets."

CHAPTER TEN

Innes

Waking up to find Kahrin already awake wasn't odd. Since they were young she'd been an 'up with the sun' person and still considered it sleeping in. The telltale trail of her things from the bed to her bag, her bag to the bathroom, and bathroom to the door meant she planned on coming back. Hopefully with breakfast. Also, that she'd taken his keys seemed a good sign.

He'd have gladly gone with her, adding exploring the neighborhood together to the other adventures of the night before, but when Kahrin put her mind to something, there was little use in talking her out of it.

So he puttered, tidying the not-quite-mess she made as she tornadoed through his little apartment. He washed up the few dishes in the sink, setting Evangeline's mug on the table so he'd remember to return it on his way out tonight.

A museum gala or something. He'd not pried too many details from Emilia before agreeing to her very specific directions on where they'd meet and what not to wear, as she'd provide anything needed further. He grinned, privately, the tingle of a thrill of adventure making him giddy in a way he was glad not to need to share with anyone right now. Not sharing it with Kahrin was new territory, even as a part of him cried out to do so. They were stumbling through a lot of that lately, weren't they?

Which had an odd way of bringing his thoughts around to Evangeline. He carefully dried and put the plates and forks away in the open-front cupboard and added cooking oil to the grocery list on his phone. He remembered her visit last night with perfect clarity but didn't remember why he'd allowed it. At the time, he'd been into it, he knew that without a doubt. His mind had raced with thoughts that weren't strictly gentlemanly, and until Kahrin had burst in, he'd been ready to act on it.

Was that what he really wanted, though? With some distance from it, and more than a few reminders that he enjoyed the carefree ties of his sex life, he could see it more clearly: no.

Evangeline, he thought, was girlfriend material. Sweet and pretty, and always offering to do nice things for him. Earnest in her want to spend time together, it often left him feeling a little guilty that he didn't want to make her more of a priority. Everything about her said she was the hapless maiden he always said he wanted, and yet? He wasn't ready to take one on.

Until she was near him, her voice as honeyed as fresh baklava and the scent about her so enticing. At those times, she filled his thoughts to distraction. Maybe, just maybe, he was thinking too practically, considering school and his job and the other activities he enjoyed all while the universe tried to give him the storybook romance he longed for.

He shook the thought away. If he wasn't sure, it wasn't fair. The most honorable thing he could do by Evangeline right now was give her his honesty.

Deciding not to wait, Innes pulled a shirt over his head and hooked the mug handle on his finger to make the trip across the hall. He wedged a sneaker in the door so he didn't lock himself out while Kahrin was gone, and rapped upon Evangeline's door.

It opened before his knuckles pulled back from it. Her pretty face lit up to see him, and once again, he felt that fuzzy warmth she brought with her everywhere.

"Innes!" She pushed the door open as far as she could reach. The long flowy pants she wore made the lines of her long legs formless and somehow still pleasing, contrasting the way her top was knotted in the back to make it tight against her flat stomach. She smoothed a wispy lock of hair back into her half ponytail as a pale pink flush spread across her cheeks. "If I'd known you'd be coming over, I'd have put on something more appropriate." She gestured to his sleep pants, and amended, "Or maybe I've stuck to the dress code."

He leaned closer, enjoying that saccharine Circus Peanut candy scent about her, similar to but more pungent than those Britney Spears perfumes Kahrin had been obsessed with in junior high. "I think you look lovely," he said honestly, forgetting the reason he was here at all.

When she beamed, he realized it didn't matter why, just that he was. She peeked out the door past his shoulder, looking up and down the hallway. "Is your, um, friend still here?" She stepped back and nodded her head inside. "Do you want to come in? I have the kettle on for tea. It'd be no problem to make another cup."

He nodded, delighted with the idea, and then heard the outer door bang shut preceding the rapid trod of feet up the stairs.

"Okay, Pretty Mouth, this is how much I love you. They didn't have your little French thing, so I got one of everything with raisins."

Oh! Kahrin! She stopped just behind him, midway in the hall.

"Oh." She frowned. "Sorry to interrupt."

He blinked, the cotton-candy feeling clearing, as well as the smile on Evangeline's face. "You didn't. I was just, um," he shook his head as he trailed off, not remembering what 'um' was meant to be followed with.

Kahrin pinged the ceramic mug with a fingernail. "Is this hers?"

"Oh! Yeah. Here." He held it out to Evangeline. "I washed it."

"Thanks." She frowned, the disappointment on her face clear, and exactly the reason he'd come over, he realized.

Kahrin rocked on her feet, then thumbed over her shoulder to show she'd be inside the apartment, but she didn't shut the door behind her.

"I don't think she likes me," Evangeline told him, attempting to keep her voice low.

He laughed. "Kahrin doesn't like anyone. Not at first." Which wasn't strictly true. She had a sliding scale of likability, and while they weren't *like that*, being interested in him lost them points almost immediately. "Don't take it personally."

Evangeline lifted and dropped her shoulder, emphasizing her sharp collarbone. "It's not her I am hoping to impress." She reached out, making a high-pitched 'boop' as she tapped his nose. Except, it felt unnatural when she did it. As if she'd seen a child do it but didn't understand why. He felt that warmth again, seeping in from his periphery. "Do you want to see a movie tonight?" she asked, to which his mind screamed that, yes, he did.

Nothing sounded more alluring than that, except maybe the possibility that they could find time alone, or a dark corner with no one else around them.

But... "I have plans tonight." Plans he was not breaking. He enjoyed these outings far too much. Which, again, was why he was here.

"With her?" She jerked her chin toward his door. Almost on cue, Kahrin dangled a scone between her fingers through the opening, reminding him he'd not yet eaten.

"I actually don't know how long she's staying." He held up her mug once more, and she took it with a quiet sigh. "I'll see you around, okay?" He smiled, stepping back from the door before turning about and making a show, as if the scent of the scone was dragging him back by the nose, for Kahrin's benefit.

"Do you want me to go?" Kahrin asked, having made herself at home and finding butter and plates. "I didn't ask before I drove in last night."

"Would it have stopped you?" Despite the dryness in his words, he grinned. He was glad she was here, and it helped him put a few things into perspective.

"Maybe if I'd known you were," she drew it out, "I don't know. Dating?"

He shook his head. "No. I think I've decided against that."

"Probably for the best." Kahrin nodded, sucking her lips over her teeth in that way he knew meant she had something she wanted to say, and was weighing how much of a row it might start.

"Out with it."

"Out with what?" Oh, the innocent act did not suit her. At all.

He sank into one of the plastic chairs and started buttering his scone. "Whatever it is you're afraid to say about Evangeline."

She scoffed, shook her head like he was insane to even suggest such a thing. When he raised his brow at her, she rolled her eyes and relented. "You need to be careful with her."

"Meaning?"

Kahrin sighed, scrutinizing her bagel as if she had a loupe held in one eye. "She doesn't like me." She held up a hand to stave off any objection that formed on his tongue about how it wasn't about her. "Which isn't the point. It's you she has to like. There's just," again with the pause as she tried to pick her words, "something different about her."

"Different, how?"

"I don't know. But I know." Which made no sense unless you were Kahrin. And he was just one or two degrees away from being Kahrin, he knew her so well. "Just watch out. This one's no unicorn."

He pointed with his lips toward her plate. "Eat your," he stopped, the conversation over as they came upon a much more disturbing topic. "Did you pick all the raisins out of that bagel?"

"Nature's boogers," she answered as she pushed them all toward him.

CHAPTER ELEVEN

Innes

Nothing about Innes' relationship with Emilia was conventional or dull, and her parties were no exception. To say she was wealthy was an understatement. If it hadn't been obvious in her series of gifts to him, the lavishness of this museum opening for one of the young artists she patronized made it so. Emilia had clawed her way up from nearly nothing and now enjoyed flaunting that success in the faces of those who'd scorned and dismissed her along the way by inviting them to her events. It gave her a carefree attitude that showed in even the slightest movement she made, exuding her cleverness and charm.

Innes played his part well: effusive and witty, and most of all, looking very handsome in her company. Such laborious work. Emilia fancied people talking about her, and keeping a young man at least twenty years her junior on her arm did the trick nicely.

"Ah!" She'd greeted him, adjusting his collar with affection, her face framed with her cropped, silver hair. "You, my handsome doctor—"

"Future doctor," he reminded her.

She waved a hand. "Details. Let's look at you." She stepped back, eyes roving with approval. "You were crafted for fine tailoring, my dear." She smiled, mirth on her lips and the usual mischief in her eyes. "I assume you found everything I sent a proper fit?"

"Yes." He blushed from the roots of his hair to his collar and resisted fidgeting. She'd not tolerate fidgeting, although that was not a very compelling reason to do as he was told. He found he often liked the consequences of bratting behavior. "I may need to burn my hard drive after looking some of it up, but I worked it out."

Her mouth curved upward but she made no comment on the, ah, accessories. She respected him, striking a delicate balance between discretion and naughtiness, with most of the fun being the stolen private moments. Honestly it made their private games more entertaining to Innes. He found unique exhilaration in her challenges. Especially one of wills.

Tonight's challenge was to speak only when spoken to, and then exclusively in the form of a question. He must have performed to her satisfaction, as he was rewarded on the drive home. Well, a little. It was hardly a surprise she enjoyed winding him up and still denying him the satisfaction.

"Your guest will not appreciate me returning you exhausted." She patted his cheek with affection and kissed him behind his jaw. "When do I get to meet her?"

"Soon," he promised. Again. "When I know how to explain it."

Emilia crooked a finger under his chin, her voice softening. "When you're ready. You know your needs will always be respected here."

He did, and he counted his stumbling into Emilia as one of the greater fortunes in his life because of it. He wished her goodnight, exiting the car and leaving the cage behind.

BLOOD OF THE TRUE BELIEVER

He couldn't believe the rattling of the keys in the lock and the horrifying screech the hinges let did not wake Kahrin when he came in the door. But there she was, underwear-clad butt in the air and face pressed into the pillows on his bed, the TV on with some made-for-TV movie that only came on late night. He slid his shoes off, using the toe of each foot to tug the opposite heel, and set the takeout box of leftover hors d'oeuvres on the little table. He tip-toed across the rug, flicking the TV off as he did, and sat on the edge of the bed beside her.

A normal person probably would have nudged her gently. Maybe tickled the bottom of her foot so they didn't get hit. Possibly even kissed her brow and murmured her name to wake her. Innes did none of that, instead immediately growling into her neck, fingers searching for her ribs in the places he knew would tickle her the most.

She thrashed about, squealing awake, one arm swinging out defensively. He caught it in his hand, laughing, and gathered her to him. "I'm home," he announced. "And you said you would wait up for me."

"You said you were going to call on your way home!" Once her initial terror had passed, she settled into annoyance, but swiftly veered into glad to see him.

"I tried, but your phone's off." He sat up, brushing hair out of her face. "I brought back food. Tiny little fancy food that's hard to pronounce and meant to be eaten without smudging lipstick."

She beamed up at him, reaching up to tug on the bowtie that dangled, unfastened, around his neck. "Apparently, that's what shirt collars are for."

"What?" He tilted his chin as Kahrin tugged at his collar, pointing out the spot, though he couldn't see it.

"Oh!" He was grateful for the low light so she wouldn't see him blush at the realization that Emilia's perfume was not the only thing lingering on his tuxedo. He pulled at the shirt, and sure enough, that was Emilia's shade. Wicked woman.

"Can't say I blame whoever it belongs to," she teased, grunting to sit up. "You clean up nice. Very nice. Where did you even get a tux?" Her brow lifted. "Big parties. Fancy clothes. You can't duck my questions about this mystery woman forever!"

"It's a long story, and not really that interesting." Which guaranteed she'd immediately press to know everything. All the more reason to lure her out of the bed and get something in her mouth. Namely the food. For now. Emilia had left him in a state, after all.

He grabbed her hand and dragged her until she had no choice but to stumble out and follow him, complaining the whole way that she just had to know. She plopped into the plastic kitchen chair, sulking, or at least pretending to, as he put the box on the table and pushed it closer to her.

"No! Leave it on!" she whined—actually whined—and kicked her feet when he unbuttoned his coat. "It's no fair that everyone else got to enjoy you all prettied up while I was here all alone."

He rolled his eyes, sitting next to her, opting not to remind her that she stayed here, so alone and bereft his company, of her very own volition. He flipped the box open as they rooted around what he'd hastily snatched up before leaving the party. Something with crostini, a few little puffs with various whipped fillings of substances that probably should not be whipped.

"Ew. What's that?" Kahrin asked, pointing at speckles

of red on a bed of creamy spread atop a slice of cucumber.

"Roe, I'm pretty sure." He offered it to her, and she recoiled as if he'd brought her raisins.

"That came out of a fish's butt." She wrinkled her nose and shook her head. "I'm not eating that."

"I think this white part is fish sperm, actually."

"That's not better!" She hopped up from the chair and went to her bag to retrieve her phone, "That's not the same thing!" She whipped around and pointed at him before he could make the obvious joke.

He shook his head, eating the cucumber himself, unsure if he appreciated the briny flavor of the fish eggs-or-whatever. Naturally, when she came back to the table, she chose his lap in lieu of her own chair, because that was the obviously the better seat. Not that he was going to complain as he got to rest his chin on her shoulder and wrap his arms around her to enjoy her warmth as she turned her phone on. At least she'd dropped the topic of Emilia. She was right though: he'd not be able to duck it for long. With either of them.

"I forgot I'd shut it off after my date." She frowned at the screen as notifications popped up in a flurry of pings and flashes.

His brow shot up. "André? Isn't that your professor?"

"Yes," she drew out before tugging her bottom lip in with her teeth to bite down on it.

He knew the answer well enough to know he didn't want to hear it, and still, he asked. "Why is your professor calling you?"

She sighed. Actually, she huffed. No wonder she'd withheld the man's name! "Probably to apologize. Or not, since he's an ass."

"You went on a date with your professor?" He frowned. "You don't think that's weird? I'm pretty sure that violates some ethics codes."

"It's fine. Probably. And irrelevant, because the date was awful, he's a dick, and I'm probably going to drop his stupid class anyway." She sagged against his chest with a theatrical groan.

Innes stroked her hair, letting his fingers pull through it down the length of her back. "How old is he?"

She tipped her chin to look up at him. "How old is Emilia?"

"Emilia is not my professor." Though, arguably she did teach him things. "Besides, we're talking about you right now, hm?"

The *hm* did it. She relented. For now. "I don't know. Thirty-something. Five? Ish?"

He dropped his head back, letting out a hard, audible breath of his own. Yet, he couldn't scold her for it at the risk of being a hypocrite, though that was still privileged information. And, it wasn't his business, not if she didn't want it to be. "Well, at least it's over, then."

She nodded. "I hate dating. It's stupid, and it's hard. I hate everyone who isn't you." Which made him chuckle. He sincerely hoped that was an exaggeration, that she wouldn't actually give up on maybe someday finding love, whatever version of that made her happy. He hadn't. He just needed more time to be ready. He had to admit, though, there was something nice about being held in such high esteem. He was only human!

There were times to be serious with Kahrin, and times to tease her. This was the latter. "Okay," he started, putting up a facade that he was drawing on infinite wisdom to now impart to her, "how about, if after you've tried everyone else, you let me know?" He ducked his head away when she reached to mess his hair. Which she predicted, going the other way with the hand behind his back. "That way I can board up the door and change my name so you don't wind up living with me."

She playfully whacked his chest. "Hilarious. We're going to live next door to one another, anyway, remember?"

"We'd kill each other."

"Convenient!" She pecked his cheek. "Because you promised we'd go together."

"Both together, or never ever," he murmured against her ear. He had a feeling he was going to be held to that promise made when they were kids. He knew he planned to hold her to it. How many life and death scenarios could two people stumble into together?

He patted her on the rump and spilled her from his lap. "I want to be comfortable, too." He undid the jacket and untucked the shirt. Kahrin helpfully hopped—yes, she actually hopped with both feet together—to him and hurried the process along. "We can find a movie to watch." He shivered as her fingers crawled up his chest, and let a less than manly squeak, squirming when she tickled him.

Changed and bundled up together on the small couch used to divide his bed from the rest of the room, he let her flip the channels until they found something they both enjoyed.

"Emilia's out of town starting next weekend, which means she won't need me to escort her."

"Oh?" She tipped her head to the side.

He held up a hand to stymie any questions he could see

brewing behind her large eyes. "She's going to Europe for a month, and I have a long weekend. So." His head bobbed back and forth, waiting for her to draw the conclusion on her own, but he could tell she was still caught up on the word 'escort.' He nudged her cheek with the tip of his nose. "We could drive out to the lake for the weekend."

"And what? Stay in one of the cabins?" She clapped her hands together, the promise of a trip together shoving his mysterious double life from her mind once more. "We could stay in one of the cabins!" She practically vibrated in his lap as she nodded, which he took to mean she agreed. "We haven't done that since my freshman year."

He knew. That was part of why he'd thought of it. "We'll see how long it takes me to throw you in the lake." He dodged as she went after his hair again.

"Joke's on you! It'll be frozen."

"Have you never gone ice fishing?"

"Innes Cameron," she scolded, "if you think I'm going to stare at a hole in the ice with you when there are many warmer and more exciting things we can do, you don't know me at all."

He hugged her close as the dramatic music crescendoed on the television. "So, polar bear swim is out, too, then?"

CHAPTER TWELVE

Kahrin

Who came up with that stupid rule that all good things had to come to an end? Kahrin wanted to give them a solid punch to the nuts. Even though many great things in her life had not come to an end—her friendship with Innes, for one—she'd known this weekend trip would eventually. She hugged Innes goodbye, hiding tears she felt stupid for crying, and left the happy little bubble they so often cohabited to drive home.

She was grateful for the quiet. Usually it vexed her, especially when she was alone...or with other people, yet here she was. No music. Just her and her thoughts and the road. Okay, she didn't have very many thoughts. Just one big thought.

She didn't like that girl, Evangeline, and she certainly did not trust her.

Whether it was jealousy at the potential of having to share her best friend's attention, greediness over this new aspect of his affections, or something in her gut she should listen to, she couldn't say, but she had to come up with a better reason to butt her nose into Innes' romantic life that didn't make her look like a jealous ex-girlfriend. Innes was a big boy. A very big boy. He could take care of himself.

Unless magic was involved.

"No," she said to no one as she shook her head. "That's ridiculous." Right? They'd already rescued a unicorn. They couldn't possibly have another strange mystical encounter with nonexistent magical beings. A moot point anyway, since if there was magic, she'd never know it. She used to think magic didn't exist. Turns out, she was the one who didn't exist to it.

A Hole in the World, Evan Greves had called her. A gap of reality where magic did not exist. If magic were vision, she was its blind spot. If it was touch, she was its neuropathy. Innes knew better than anyone about magical things and fantasy, and if there was something fantastic about Evangeline other than her willowy height and pretty smile, he'd see it. Or so she had to believe, if she was going to make it back to school instead of turning this car around.

School. That's what required her focus right now. Her energy had to be spent getting through her day a little tired, and a little agitated at having to start out her week in André's presence.

He watched her walk in. Kahrin kept her eyes from meeting his, though she could feel them boring through her as she took her seat. She kept her head down through the lecture, taking notes furiously to keep herself focused. All she had to do was survive the hour and she could be on her way.

Life, however, was not that kind. The end of Kahrin's braid caught in the back of the chair as she jumped up, sending her books and paper scattering and taking her and her chair to the ground with a crash. Thankfully, unlike high school, no one here found it necessary to applaud her on her dive, leaving her to her embarrassment and wishing she'd just burst into flames.

"Let me help with that," André offered, crouching to pick up her things as she disentangled her hair from the bolt on the bottom of the chair. "Are you all right?"

"I'm fine," she snapped. She snatched her notes and pens from him and stuffed them into her bag with a grunt and having no care for how they crumpled. "Professor."

His lips thinned into a line as he stood, offering her book back to her as the last student left them alone. "I feel terrible about what happened the other night."

"Nothing happened." She zipped her bag and looked him dead in the eyes. "I ditched you, remember? Have an outstanding day." She turned on heel and toe before striding purposefully away.

"I should have asked what was bothering you," he called, stopping her just before she could cross the threshold. "You're her, aren't you?"

Kahrin spun about and glared. "Her *who*?"

"The high school girl who was stabbed out there a few years ago. With her boyfriend."

"Best friend," she corrected. Shaking her head she turned to leave, then spun right back in. "How do you know about that?"

André, certain he was as cute as he thought he was, grinned. "It's a small town, Miss Quirke."

"Stop that," she hissed.

"Stop what?" Oh, he was not pulling that *I'm so innocent* act with her. She invented that act! Or at least improved upon the method.

"That cute little shit thing you're doing. It's not, and I'm better at it than you'll ever be." She strode out the door, sneakers squeaking on the tiled floor before she whipped around once more and stomped back in. "And it's Kahrin.

We went on a date; stop acting like you're at all an appropriate person."

André crossed his arms, the corners of his mouth twitching as he fought a smile. To his credit, he at least pretended to take this seriously. "You're right."

"Of course—" *Wait, what?* She lifted a brow, trying to regain the wind he'd just knocked out of her. "I know I am. I don't need you to tell me." Forgetting the fact that he was her professor, sure, and that, yeah, it was his job to tell her things she did not know. In *an appropriate setting*, she couldn't help adding to her thought, and jerked her chin, happy to have her moral high ground again. Even if he couldn't hear her reclaim it.

"I didn't know about the quonsets." He lifted a hand in an *oh, well* gesture. "Not for sure, anyhow."

"That doesn't sound like an apology." She rocked on her feet, trying to maintain her agitation as she felt her fury soften.

He shrugged. "It's not. How could I have known what you were upset about if you didn't tell me?" Her lips pressed tight together as she had to concede he had a point. She'd not used her words. Amazingly people who were not Innes had not developed the talent of reading her mind. "I'd like to make it up to you."

"You want to make something up to me that you're not sorry for?" Her expression flickered from irritated to confused and finally to something akin to being pleased for his attention. Even if she hated that she liked it. This guy was an *ass*, almost twice her age, insistent, and more than a little arrogant. She should have been incredibly creeped out, especially considering the older men before him that she'd...well she still wasn't sure. Crush seemed wrong, and attraction wasn't exactly it, as part of her had remained equally repulsed by Evan. And that grandpa who'd nearly hit her with his car? What was he even? Irrelevant, that's what. What was relevant was what she wanted to do right now. Only, she didn't know what that was.

"Have dinner with me." She tilted her chin to let him know that was a decent start. "We'll go somewhere well lit, yet still romantic. We'll talk. We can go from there." He stepped a little closer, his smile going crooked in a way that almost made him boyish. "I had a really great end for the night picnic planned. Perhaps we could resurrect it?"

Kahrin felt herself snatch a breath over her teeth and forgot to let it out. There went her belly, flipping over and sending a warmth through her. For each part of her that found his attention pleased her there was another part of her screaming that this was a terrible idea.

"Well you're optimistic. How'd that work out for you?"

He rolled and dropped his shoulders, the very picture of someone who didn't believe they'd done anything wrong. This time when he stepped closer, she lifted her chin. Defiant? Inviting? She wasn't sure. She didn't care. Dammit.

"Maybe you could tell me at dinner?" Oh, how her stupid head spun with what a stupid idea this was, and that was exactly why she wanted it.

"I could give you a preview," he murmured, the warm timbre of his voice making her flush as he leaned down the considerable distance, stopping just short of her mouth. He pushed the door shut. "If you'd like."

She swallowed, her remaining shreds of good sense reminding her that this was not the way a student and her teacher were supposed to interact with one another. A fact which did very little to sway her to the side of good choices. She tipped her face up, closing the distance, and took the kiss he dangled in front of her. It was all the encouragement he needed as he immediately overwhelmed her, wrapping his arms tight around her until she dropped her bag. He swept her backward until she felt the wall against her spine. Oh, anyone could walk in at any time, and that made it all the better. Not that she wanted someone to see them, that would be terrible! But the risk was there, and that's what she wanted. The risk.

She looped her arms around his neck, noting the taste of coffee on his tongue and the smell of a cologne she didn't quite like but really didn't hate, either. She held tight, warmth flooding her instantly, and she whimpered into it. Soft, but no less needy.

Shaking her head, she pushed away with hands between them against his chest, trying to catch her breath. She swallowed, a little dizzy, and looked up to meet his eyes. They were crinkled at the corners, like he had some kind of secret, which should have made ice harden her stomach. The last time someone looked at her like that, he did have a secret, and it was nearly a deadly one. Instead, it made the bottom of her stomach drop out, and she bit her swollen lip. "Okay. Let's have dinner," she breathed.

He didn't say anything else as she stooped to pick up her bag, slinging it over her shoulder. He simply walked back to the table to begin packing up his things and closing down the computer. She got as far as the door before looking over her shoulder at him, just to see if he was going to watch her and her cute butt leave. He didn't look up, remaining focused on his task as if she'd never been there.

This was a very, very bad idea.

CHAPTER THIRTEEN

Kahrin

This should have been our first date, Kahrin thought, looking around the small, dimly lit little bistro, a fair drive out of town. With the charming half-burnt candles sticking out of brightly colored bottles and dripping hot rivulets of wax down the sides. A scattering of other couples bent over other tables. No two chairs at any table matched, and the tablecloths all looked like they were from a church rummage sale run by her Ma. It wasn't anywhere as fancy as the place she'd been to with...whatever his name was, but she thought it was much nicer. The water came to the table in stoppered bottles, and even though it was just regular tap water the waiter poured it into fancy stemmed glasses.

André offered to buy her a drink, but she declined. He only kind of teased her for it. He ordered for her—grilled octopus—and when she didn't like it, he only kind of teased her for it. It wasn't a total loss, since he let her choose the dessert.

"Did I tell you about the time I went backpacking through Europe?" The conversation flowed well enough. He liked to talk about himself, but that wasn't so bad. "I had just finished my undergrad."

She shook her head. He'd actually seen and done things,

not having lived in this boring backwater his whole life. He already knew the public version of the most interesting thing that happened to her, and there were only so many stories a person could tell about running before the topic grew tedious. It wasn't hard to be interested in someone who had done actual interesting things.

"You're athletic." Hardly a deep observation, with her defined muscles, but she'd allow it. "You might enjoy something like that. Seeing the world out there past state lines."

"I've always wanted to travel." Which was at least partially true. She did want to leave this town, someday. She showed her eyeteeth with the smile that stretched her face. "And who's going to take me on this fantastic trip? You?"

"I thought we were only going to plan on dinner."

She laughed now and tucked a strand of dark hair behind her ear. "Touché."

"Are you nervous?" He grinned over his glass of wine, which had stained a small line in the dry skin of his lower lip.

She shook her head. "Why?"

"You've been bouncing your leg." He nodded as she looked to see that she was, in fact, bobbing the foot which was not tucked beneath her.

"I'm not one for sitting still." She shrugged, sucking some of the syrup off of her spoon.

"I've noticed that. In class." He laughed into his glass. "You're always moving."

She tensed, both hands on the bowl of her water glass. "Can we not...talk about my habits as your student?" She smiled, trying to make it genuine, but finding it tight, all the same.

"Are you embarrassed?" Was she? Should she be? "What's there to be embarrassed about?" He sat back and looked at her from under the lids of his eyes, managing to seem as if she was the only other person in the room. "We're two adults on a date."

This time, her smile was more strained. "I know." As he kept reminding her of the fact that she was an adult. Just like him. For some reason, the more he asserted it, the less amusing she found it. "I also know how pretty I am. I dressed myself so I know I look nice." He lifted an eyebrow. "What I'm saying is you don't have to waste time stating obvious things."

He laughed, now, a little too loud for the soft string music being piped over the restaurant radio. "You don't think that's a little arrogant?"

"No." Her brow pinched, mouth pulled up on once side. "How is that arrogant? You tell me I'm pretty, and I'm supposed to thank you, but it's not okay if I already know I'm pretty?" She leaned forward, cupping one hand around her mouth as if sharing a secret. "We call that a double standard. And, bee tee dubs, I'm not pretty. I'm hot." Of the two of them at the table, she was the one who'd bothered to dress nice—a tunic sweater over skinny jeans with a soft scarf—when he looked not unlike he'd just come in from that hike through Europe. It wasn't a bad look on him, but he didn't *look* like he was going out for a date.

"That's what I like about you," he started, resting the foot of his glass on the table. "You say whatever pops into your head."

Okay. She had to give him that one, and lightly rolled her shoulders, having no better answer for that. Time to change the subject away from herself. "What made you decide to teach science?"

"I teach anatomy." She nodded, not sure what difference it made. She ran middle and long distance but sprinters were still runners. "I like the order of it all. The way everything works together, beautiful in its simplicity despite how complex it all is." He handed his card to the waiter without looking up.

"Kind of like magic, right? That's why I—"

"No, it's not magic. The body is designed deliberately. Take your running, for example. Your hips and legs are held together by tendons and ligaments, defining your gait, but also limited by them because of the purpose of your reproductive system." He gestured to her vaguely.

"What does that mean?"

"You're designed to birth children, so your stride is inefficient," he went on. "There's nothing magic about that."

She stood up from the table. "Yeah, but you don't believe that. Right?"

"Believe what? Science?"

"No, in all that stuff about," she waved her hand in a circle as she reached for words. "The purpose of bodies. Blah blah have babies because that's what your body is for."

"Will you sit down? You're making a scene."

She blinked, an argument on her tongue that died faster than it could connect to her brain. "Will you take me back to my car? Please?"

Sliding his card back in his wallet and jamming it in his pocket, he stood. "Now what's wrong?"

Gesturing around the room to indicate their audience, some who were now looking at them, she shook her head to let him know that, no, they were not doing this here. "I want to leave, André."

"Fine." He stood, letting her go ahead of him as they made their way outside and back to his car. "I don't know what you're so angry about," he continued as they walked toward his car. Kahrin hugged her arms around herself against the cold, glancing up to him, her jaw set in agitation. "I'm not saying you want to drop out of school and have babies now. You're only twenty."

She stopped walking. "What does my age have to do with anything?"

"You're way too young to make that decision yet," he said casually as he opened the car door for her.

She stopped. "So, what, I'm too young to know what I want to do with my body, but I'm mature enough to fuck you? Is that it?"

"What is wrong with you?" he demanded, lifting a hand flat in front of himself. "You're not like this in class."

"We're not *in* class. You're not my teacher here." Her hands waved wildly around. "And I don't want babies."

"No, of course not."

"Ever," she emphasized. "I don't want them ever." He opened his mouth and she cut him off. "I don't even have a uterus. I had to decide," *where I could get stabbed and live*, "some things, and I chose to let that go, because I didn't plan to use it."

André ran a hand over his face and muttered something which sounded like it could have been an apology. "Why are we even talking about this? No one is asking you to have children right now. Especially not me. I—" he waved his hand and took a breath. A deep one, holding it a moment, then letting it out hard and recollecting his smile and demeanor. "We were having a nice time, I thought."

Until he started being an ass. Sure. "We were." She ran a hand over her hair, willing to concede she'd overreacted. "Are. I don't...can we just reset or something?"

"Reset?" The corner of his mouth twitched upward. "Like, we pretend the conversation never happened?"

"Sort of." She smiled, feeling a touch of shyness she was unaccustomed too. "And then we keep going with our plans for the night." Her fingers found the hem of her tunic and began twisting it. "Like magic."

He rolled his dark eyes. "Like adults. There's no such thing as magic."

She opened her mouth to argue, but stopped. When had she started getting offended when people didn't believe? Instead, she stayed on topic. "So...your place or mine?" She was, of course, joking. She lived with her parents and slept on a trundled daybed.

Which was probably why she did not expect his answer. "Let's do yours. Mine's...a mess. I won't stay long." He stepped closer to her, pulling her flush with him. "Just long enough." He ducked his head and stole a kiss, his lips shaping to hers enough to make her lament his pulling away.

She shivered, forgetting the whole fight altogether. Maybe not all together, but it didn't seem to matter so much right now, with the promise of his mouth on hers dangling in front of her. "Okay," she relented. "But my parents are home, and you don't get to meet them."

He chuckled softly, brushing his lips over her cheek, her neck, anywhere he could gain access to skin. "They won't even know I'm there."

So, she got into the car, happy to have salvaged the night.

CHAPTER FOURTEEN

Innes

Innes made a conscious effort to pull his hand out of his hair, where his forehead had been resting against it as he worked out the formula on his Biochemistry exam. All the studying in the world wouldn't help if he hadn't slept enough, and right now he did not feel like there was actually enough sleep left in the world.

He scrubbed at his eyes, looked up at the clock, then back to his booklet. His mind spun with everything except the solution. The squeaky hinges on his apartment door. Needing to check the oil in his car before driving home over the weekend. How he had trouble shaking Evangeline out of his head when he'd made up his mind about her. The fact that Kahrin went on another date with that ass. And last, but certainly not least, what was so urgent that Emilia needed to see him before she left town? Not that he'd dare question it, and not as if she'd forbid him to speak the entire month she was away. That would be excessive, even for her games.

He was about ninety-nine per cent sure of that one.

He dropped his head back and exhaled at the ceiling, letting his eyes unfocus and then refocus on the little smattering of decorative holes in the tiles there. He glanced at the clock once more as he sat back up, but this time when he looked down at his test, the answer came to him, and he hurried to finish his work.

His feet found the floor and the test was in his hand before he stood, dropping his pencil into his bag and hurrying to turn it in. He was halfway to the door before the Grad Assistant called him back to put his name on his booklet. He wrote it as neatly as his haste would allow, and was out the door.

The one good advantage to such pricey rent for his lowly efficiency was the very short drive to school and back, though it was a much longer bus ride. Hence the car. He parked, then took his stairs two at a time to the top, checking his watch to make certain he wasn't late. He made it to the door just in time, swinging his bag inside it, then pulling it closed and standing in front of it, waiting. He shuffled his weight from leg to leg, trying to look casual, less like he was standing at attention, but the more he tried to look casual, well, that didn't need explaining. He checked his watch once more. It was unlike Emilia to be late for anything she did not intend to be fashionably late to.

"Are you waiting for a woman?" Innes turned his head toward the stairs at the other end of the hall to see the burnished copper of Evangeline's hair in the late afternoon sun filtered through the windows. "Older? Cropped grey hair? Well-dressed?"

That was Emilia. Had he gotten the time wrong? He didn't answer, not quite knowing how. He wasn't ready to tell Kahrin the ins and outs of his relationship with Emilia; he certainly was not going to tell anyone else.

Turned out he didn't need to. "She was here. I thought it was weird that she let herself in. Is she your aunt?"

"Oh, no. A friend." He turned around to head inside.

"Thank you. Saves me waiting."

"You know," Evangeline said, catching his attention once more. She tilted her head, hair tumbling down her shoulder as if it were styled just for that purpose in this moment. "She's not very friendly. She left quickly when I introduced myself." That didn't sound like Emilia. Strange.

"Um, thanks." Thanks for what? He didn't know. He met Evangeline's warm eyes, caught up in them for the space of a slow breath. He felt himself lean in her direction, pulled by a cord he couldn't see with a tensile strength he didn't understand. If it hadn't been for the overwhelming curiosity of what Emilia had gotten up to in his apartment, he might have forgotten he was doing anything at all.

"I'll talk to you later," he said with an owlish expression. Evangeline's brow creased when he shook out of his daze and waved to her, indicating he was going inside. She strode toward him, her body coiled with agitation to the point he thought she might lunge at him, the limp in her step more pronounced. She didn't attack him, at least not in the way he foolishly expected and even braced for.

Her mouth was on his, scent and taste overwhelming his senses instantly. It was oddly warm, even for a kiss, but a hint of sugar lingered on her tongue as she teased it past his lips. It didn't take long to give in. Why would it? He was only a man, and a beautiful woman was kissing him with a hungry ferocity. His arms circled around her thin waist. His fingers followed the ridge of every bone of her spine as they moved up over her sweater. He felt dizzy, the whole world being her and her alone now. He couldn't even remember what he'd been doing before this kiss, and had no idea what he intended to do after. He needed a moment to collect his thoughts. But her hands were on his chest, and she made a sound like water steaming out of a burning log. In the back of his mind was a voice—Emilia's voice—reminding him to be clear about what he needed.

He pushed her back, gently. "I need a moment. Please." He chuckled softly, then cleared his throat. "I was in the middle of something, and—"

Evangeline pouted, but nodded, backing up half a step. Even still, something danced in her eyes, the light making them look like molten bronze for an instant. "Let's go inside, Innes." Her fingers wound into his, hot to the touch, but he barely noticed. She slipped her other arm past his waist and pushed his door open. "Someone might see us."

Well, of course he didn't want that! He nodded, backing into his apartment, unable to recall why he'd ever stopped her before. "I don't want that," he repeated his thoughts aloud.

"Me neither." One of her hands pushed the door closed behind them, the other threading up into his hair at the back of his neck. He didn't let people touch his hair, except for...for...he couldn't remember her name. This time, when Evangeline locked her mouth on his, he lost his breath, his entire chest emptying out and he forgetting how to draw it back in again. He let her push him further, urging him back, around the small couch that divided the room, until he felt the mattress of his bed touch the backs of his legs. She pulled at his shirt, making him angry at it for being in her way. Her mouth was everywhere, singeing a line over the apple of his throat, to his collarbone, leaving him certain he would find sear marks left behind.

"I was beginning to think you didn't want me," she coaxed softly in his ear. She nipped the place where his jaw met below his ear, pressing one leg between both of his. "Good to know I was wrong."

Her hands gripped his, almost too tight for his liking, but he didn't fight it. Innes let himself be pushed back, keeping one arm about her waist to avoid the excruciating thought of being denied her. He stumbled past the stand near the bed, and something clattered to the floor. As much as his body screamed for him to just ignore it, the mental fog scattered. Evangeline flicked her tongue over the small bare patch of skin on his jaw, which was the last thing to bring him to his senses. He jerked his head away, hating the way it felt for her to even touch that sacred spot on his jaw.

He stepped back to put space between them, pushing gently with both of his hands flat on her shoulders. "Evangeline, we need to stop. Please." He blinked rapidly, whatever happened between the door and here lost in a swirling mist which was surely the daze of their making out making him see things. "I'm sorry." His eyes settled on the box as he stooped to retrieve it. The craftsmanship of the vessel was artfully made, carved out of a single piece of wood, judging by the grain, and polished glossy. A newer and more ornate version of the sort of thing Kahrin had kept trinkets in when they were children, made by her Da. There was no question who the gift was from. It had Emilia written all over it. Well, apart from it being on the floor and splayed open.

"I don't understand the problem, Innes."

His eyes looked up, as if seeing Evangeline for the first time. For one moment he could swear that smoke floated up and away from her hair as the late sun shone off of it. "I don't, either," he murmured as he picked up the box.

What was inside didn't help his confusion. At least, not as to what Evangeline was doing here, or the need for this gift to be in such an ornate package. Folded very neatly inside the velvet lined box was a small blue cloth with an impossibly delicate trim of handmade lace. It was as exquisite as it was obviously old, and on one corner a little white flower, shaped like droplets, had been embroidered. He thought he recalled from stories it being a snowdrop, though he'd never seen a real one.

Innes fingered it with a gentle touch, an affectionate twist of smile crinkling his eyes. He'd received some strange and often interesting gifts from Emilia, but his wildest imagination could not conjure a reason for this. It was possible that the small note sealed in an envelope would explain, but it was not a given. He set it back in its place and straightened the lid, checking it for damage.

Evangeline's lips curled downward at the sight of the handkerchief and she stepped away as if it were a dead rat about to come back to life and attack her.

"I thought you were into it," she explained, a coolness in her voice that had not been there moments ago. "I wouldn't have let it get this far if I knew otherwise."

Innes looked up at her, confused, both by her tone and her expression. Her anger rolled off in palpable waves, and Innes felt shame crawl over him. This was not the sort of gallant way maidens were treated by heroes in stories. "I'm really sorry. I don't know what came over me. The last thing I want to do is hurt you."

"I have to go," she answered simply, turning on one foot and hurrying out the door without looking back.

CHAPTER FIFTEEN

Kahrin

"Shh!" Kahrin giggled behind her sealed lips, hoping like she'd never hoped before that her parents were both sound asleep. "No, no, you can't leave your shoes there," she chastised André. "What if my Da has to go outside? He'll notice extra shoes." That weren't Innes'. She assumed. Actually, Kahrin had never snuck anyone into her room. She'd never had to, as the only boy she'd ever thought to bring up there was her best friend, who had an open invite.

"You're serious?" he asked, his whisper cutting through the distance between them. "What am I, a high school boy?" Even as his words were resentful, the soft laugh from his throat was not.

"Only as serious as your self-preservation." Her warning showed on her face, and he shook his head and picked up his shoes. "Which is going to need to be epic if you wake my mother."

She pulled him by the hand, from the mudroom and through the dining room, around and up the stairs, stepping carefully in the places she knew the stairs didn't creak. Brecken and Alec were both gone, so she didn't worry about knocking at their door as they passed through her brothers' room to her own little alcove.

"Why do you still live with your parents?" he asked,

ducking his head to avoid hitting the slanted ceiling. It was more than a little disconcerting, the way he implied there was something wrong with that fact.

"Because not all of us are college professors." Obviously. "Also, my parents need my help with things sometimes, and it's easier if I'm just here."

"Is that a daybed?" he asked, utterly puzzled by the sight of it.

She nodded, self-consciousness tightening her shoulders with each question. "It has a trundle. I'm not a large person. It fits me." He shook his head, resigned, though it didn't stop him from grabbing her around the waist and pulling her to him. He kissed her, hard and without preamble, like he was on the clock and would turn into a pumpkin if they wasted too much time.

Kahrin's heart hammered, but she wasn't sure it was all good. Was this what she wanted? Sneaking a man into the house, whimpering for more as he pulled her clothes away until they were skin against skin, at least from the waist up. André looked down to her, the light from the outdoor floods backlighting him so that his face was dark but his hair stood, a mass of messy flames in contrast to the rest.

She tipped her chin as he began exploring her neck, his lips murmuring compliments she didn't care about and other nonsense as he drew her down, pressing his weight against her onto the trundle.

The trundle.

"Stop."

André froze in place, his hands lifting from her right away. "What is it?" He rocked back to sitting on his knees. "What's wrong?"

"No—nothing's wrong, really." She crossed her arms over her chest, suddenly shy and more aware of her nakedness than ever in her life, and hopped up from the bed. "I just can't...here."

"In your own room?" That drop in tone of his voice was there again. Judging her and challenging her.

"No." Well, yes. With her parents sleeping down the hall. "Just...here. In this bed. It's...it's silly. Well, not silly. I mean it matters. To me." She shook her head as she stood and backed away. "That's Innes' bed."

"Who?" Even in the dark she could see his eyes narrow.

"Does it matter?" A spike of defensiveness rose in her and she had to take a deep breath to keep from raising her voice.

André huffed. Actually huffed. He ran a hand over his face as he stood. "Look, if you're not into this, just say so. I'm not looking to play games with a flighty girl."

"Now I'm a flighty girl?" Kahrin's face hardened. "Well, I'm sorry that having sex in my best friend's bed bothers me. Didn't mean to ruin your night."

"You didn't ruin my night. This is your room and..." A grunt rolled up from his throat. "I'm sneaking into someone's house like a teenager."

"Yeah, well, if you recall, I was a teenager last year." She walked across the floor and gathered up his shoes, sweatshirt, and body warmer. "I'm guessing math isn't your specialty."

"Kahrin, what are you doing? Don't act like this."

She crossed the floor of her room, the slanted ceiling just the right height for her as she unlocked and slid the window open. A blast of cool air puffed snow over her, prickling her skin and further clarifying the absurdity of the moment. "Like what? This?" She tossed his things out the window, then stepped further into the slant as he hit his head trying to rush to her, as if he could stop what already happened.

"What is wrong with you?" he demanded, rubbing his head with one hand and lifting the other arm.

"Me? I'm not the old guy here chasing a much younger woman and then complaining about her maturity." She flapped her hands at the window. "Have a good night, André."

He blinked. "What?"

"Get out."

"Out the window? You're joking."

"Mm, nope." She dug her pajamas out from under her pillow and pulled the oversized shirt over her head. Emboldened with her remembered modesty, she stepped toward him, blocking his way to the rest of the room as if she wasn't small enough for him to lift out of the way with even his skinny arms. "Out you go." She paused, her face hard and expectant. "Before I show you how immature I can be and scream for my father."

André held both hands up, swearing under his breath as he climbed out. "Great. Just great."

"Good night!" She didn't watch to see if he made it down. As soon as his fingers were off the ledge, she shut the pane and locked it once more, then drew the curtains closed. Somehow, she didn't feel enraged. Cold calm, yes, but also something else. Some kind of flip and twist in her stomach that felt oddly good. After pushing the trundle back in, she burrowed into her own bed, pulling the blankets tight around her chin and closed her eyes.

Tossing and turning a few times, she finally gave up

and hopped out of bed. She yanked the trundle out and before it even locked in place, she tore the bedding from it, wadding it up in an angry ball of sheets and quilt. She hauled it down the stairs to the mudroom, cramming it all in the washer, not even caring that it was a little too much for one load. She stayed up, watching some stupid movie with a plot she didn't care about but entertaining her long enough to put the bedding in the dryer after. Just as she was getting drowsy, she heard the dryer buzz, and went to gather them up. Her bare feet made soft thuds on the stairs as she carried it all back up and remade the trundle.

There. All better.

This time when she slid into her own bed, the trundle tucked back into place beneath hers, she didn't have any trouble falling asleep.

She didn't think about André when she got up, or when she took her run. In fact she hit a personal best for the five she covered. She didn't give him another thought as she showered and pulled on enough clothing to make herself modest before going down to meet her parents at the breakfast nook. Ma bustled about, mixing dried blueberries into the oatmeal, which sounded unusually good to her.

She was midway through a drink of orange juice when Da took his seat across from her. "Where is your guest?"

She managed not to spit, but wound up choking on it instead. Once she cleared her throat and recovered enough to talk, her eyes met Da's, very much like her own, but more even in color. "Hm?"

Ma sank down into the chair beside them. "The man whose footprints, I assume, were the ones in the snow leading away from beneath your window."

"Oh." She pursed her lips in thought. She couldn't talk

her way out of this, and decided not to even try. "He couldn't stay."

Da lifted his brows, taking a deep draft of his coffee.

"Why not?" Ma asked, and Kahrin recognized that she was not asking because she had a burning need to fix him a bowl of porridge.

"I didn't let him," she replied, simply, digging into her oatmeal. "I changed my mind about him."

Da stood, sliding his chair back in and carrying his bowl and mug to the sink. "Come out to the south field before dinner and find me, *makoons*."

Great. She nodded at her breakfast. She didn't need to say anything, and wouldn't dare mouth off. Da wanted to *talk*, which was decidedly different from talking. Ma stood and kissed him goodbye, lingering a little longer than Kahrin had stomach for. It did make her chuckle with affection, lightening her mood to see her parents still very much in love. Maybe a little too in love, if such a thing existed. "I'll be there."

CHAPTER SIXTEEN

Innes

It didn't make sense. He shopped at a grocery store, had their free loyalty card, which was already ridiculous. Why did you need a loyalty card? Why not just give the same lowered prices to everyone, since just about everyone had the card to begin with? But then, they add a phone app. 'To get the most out of your card savings,' it said. That made even less sense. Yet, here Innes stood, swiping through the nearly endless page of coupon ads to make sure he got the best discounts on the items that were already marked down for everyone who asked for the free card anyhow. He couldn't imagine being his brother Brodie's wife, searching every mailer and flyer for deals and going to three stores to get the best prices. He missed the days when Ma Quirke just fed him and he didn't have to do his own shopping. Part of growing up. Part of being independent.

He actually suspected if he asked Ma Quirk for help packing for the weekend, she'd have done it gladly. He could have taken Emilia's offer to have one of the cabins stocked before he and Kahrin arrived there. Kindness was one thing, but depending on people to take care of him was not how he wanted to live his life. Not the type of man he wanted to be.

Besides, he had a much more arduous task ahead of

him: making certain there were things Kahrin would actually eat while they were on their trip. She wasn't so finicky that she was impossible to feed, and her parents wouldn't allow waste besides, but now that she was old enough to decide what she wanted, she was very adamant about what she did not want.

He crouched as he inspected the bananas, trying to determine which would be ripe to eat over the weekend and which ones were trying to deceive him. Dodgy things, bananas. Definitely the trickster of the fruit world. They were good at guarding an empty stomach for a run, though, and he hadn't met Kahrin just last week. He had no delusions that he would be sleeping past sunrise and avoiding those early morning runs with her.

He saw Evangeline out of the corner of his eye before she spoke. "You take bananas very seriously."

"You should see my painstaking choosing of carrots." He smiled crookedly, feeling a little foolish and just grabbing a bunch which seemed reasonably green. "I didn't know you shop here." What? He could have smacked himself in the face.

"At the only store in walking distance from our apartment building?" Her thin pink lips fought a smile as she held up her hand basket. "Just a few necessities." She peered into his cart. "Is there an incoming blizzard?"

"What?" He glanced down. It was really a lot for just one person. "Oh, no. I'm going away this weekend."

"Really?" Surprise in her voice was underscored by the raise of her pale ginger brows. "I thought you were so busy you didn't have time to go out."

Oh. Ouch. Innes ducked his head, rubbing his hand over the back of his hair. She was right. He had said that. Of course he prioritized Kahrin without thinking anything of it. "Just some nice quiet time with my best friend." Of course, 'quiet' and 'Kahrin' didn't work together in one sentence, but some of what he had in mind didn't need both. Not a given, but he had noted a trend, and was curious to see if it maintained, uh, course.

"The one who was visiting before?" She frowned in a way that made Innes uncomfortable, though he couldn't say why. It wasn't jealousy, but it was something.

"The very same." He started pushing his cart, indicating with a nod of his head that she was welcome to join him as they shopped. He veered his cart in the direction of the breakfast aisle, ready to debate with himself the finer points of pancake mix versus the ingredients to make them from scratch. "We grew up together. When I moved away, it was a big change for both of us." He'd not thought of how it might look from the outside, because it was so normal to them.

"Oh." That was all she said as she examined a box of marshmallow-laden cereal. "Well. Okay. That sounds fun."

A heavy quiet hung between them as he opted for the box of mix that would also work for making biscuits and pushed on. Evangeline walked along, her slim hips slightly crooked—not that he was looking—as she held her basket in front of her with both hands. She didn't say anything else until they reached snack foods and he was weighing the pros and cons of getting those not-onion onion rings Kahrin liked that made her breath stink.

"Did I...do something wrong?"

He looked over at her, the risk analysis of Kahrin's breath forgotten for the moment. "Why would you think that?"

"It's nothing." She waved a hand. "I'm being too sensitive."

"Tell me?" he prompted, folding his arms over the handle of the cart and giving her his full attention.

"I like you." She laid it out blunt, leaving no room for misinterpretation, even over something she'd made abundantly clear in the past. "I'm pretty sure a corpse could have figured it out by now, considering." Innes tried not to laugh, not wanting to be glib, but he chuckled with an awkward warmth crawling over his face. "You...kind of avoid me. And then the other day." She tipped her head as if it pained her to bring up.

"Look, I'm–I'm sorry about the other day. I've been—"

"Busy. I know." She smiled at him, her lips tucked tight as she lifted and dropped bony shoulders. "And I understood when you told me that before. You even said you'd let me know if you freed up your schedule. And then that kiss happened."

He did say that, and he did do that, and he dropped his gaze for a moment. He didn't really consider this trip a matter of his schedule being freed. More like a long overdue chance to really spend time with his best friend. They both had a lot to talk about, and, selfishly, he wanted her undivided attention for a little while. He was certain she was feeling the same since her last date with *André*. "Look, it's not like that."

"I know. You keep saying."

He shook his head. "No, I mean, Kahrin," *saved my life*, "is my best and oldest friend. This is important. I am busy, I just," he trailed off, trying to think of a way to explain it without sounding mean. It wasn't that he couldn't make time for dates. Emilia would never put such limitations on his time. The truth was he liked his time with Emilia, the adventures she enjoyed dressing him up for, and the many, many things she taught him. And his time with Kahrin? "Kahrin's nonnegotiable."

Evangeline dropped her head and nodded, lips pinched as she muttered, "Okay."

His chest squeezed, leaving him feeling like an ass. He'd not meant to hurt her feelings, even understanding there was really no avoiding it in this situation, and that was his fault. He scuffed his boot against the floor. "Are you...doing anything right now?"

She held her basket up in front of her, giving him a look that the answer should have been obvious.

He chuckled, some of the tension lifting. "We could finish our shopping together and then," he shrugged, "get juice or something?" It was harmless and noncommittal. Something even friends would do.

"Juice?" She laughed as she stepped forward and put her basket into his cart. "Are you seven? I thought most adults drink coffee."

"I like juice." He grinned, rolling his eyes. "Coffee, then. Whatever you like."

Evangeline sauntered closer, fiddling with a button on his flannel shirt. The usual rush of senses that came with her proximity didn't flood him. "This is a college town. I'm sure there's a juice bar. I bet some of them even still have straws." Her eyes fell on the pocket of his shirt and her smile vanished. "What's that?"

"Hm?" He glanced down to where the little blue handkerchief was folded in his pocket, just as Emilia had instructed: the snowdrop facing forward. He didn't always understand her games, but if Emilia told him he was to keep it on him at all times, then keep it with him he would. "Oh. It's kind of like a bet. It's a really long story."

Evangeline's nostrils flared, though her mouth still curved upward, the smile not meeting her eyes. She lifted her basket from his cart once more. "You know, I just remembered that I have something I need to do. Rain check?"

Innes blinked, the shift in her mood leaving him whiplashed. He'd done something wrong, but couldn't say what. The hanky was a little silly, but it wasn't that bad. Was it Kahrin? There was nothing to be done about that, as he'd already made clear.

"Sure," he answered. "Of course." He waved, halfheartedly and helpless as she walked off. At the end of the aisle she put her basket on the floor and quickened her steps toward the exit.

CHAPTER SEVENTEEN

Kahrin

Kahrin hadn't been ordered out to the field to talk to Da in a few years. She'd sought him out from time to time on her own when she needed advice, but usually when she required a talking to, Ma was sufficient. Ma possessed an uncanny ability to make you want to sink into the floor until God couldn't see you anymore. If Kahrin hadn't known about her unique magical resistance, she might have thought it was some sort of mind control.

Only for the most serious offenses did a Quirke sibling get summoned to Da while he was in the field. The fact that Ma packed them a snack did nothing to assuage Kahrin's trepidation. That meant they were expected to be there awhile. Ma offered no hint as to what awaited her in the south field, another detail which did nothing to put her anxiety at ease. That was likely intentional. Maybe Ma did possess some kind of magic after all. No, Kahrin would definitely know by now.

Bundled in her barn coat and ear warmer, Pickle trotting dutifully behind her, Da wasn't difficult to find. Being winter, the field stood bare save for the stray raspy stalk of whatever had grown the previous season poking up through the snow. Da had the goats out to run as he knelt by the perimeter fence. Pickle bounded off, both announcing their arrival (as if Da didn't hear them coming), and running alongside the fence looking for a way into the field.

"I come bearing refreshments," she said. She held the insulated lunch pack out in front of her like an offering of peace. Da faced her with a turn of his head and nodded with his lips toward the nearby truck, tailgate folded down. Without argument, Kahrin led the way, pulling herself up onto the gate with all the grace of a swimmer pushing themselves out of the deep end of the pool. Even Da had to hop a little to get up beside her with the lunchbox. Side by side they cut a striking resemblance, at least in appearance.

Twitchy and chatty since forever, it always took Kahrin great patience to wait on Da to speak his mind. He had the unsettling ability to go still until you thought he was asleep or maybe had turned to stone. Even his breathing was silent, the only proof of it the plumes of mist that rose from his mouth and nose. She did her best not to fidget, knowing this was a test. Da demanded attention and patience for these talks, and did not so much as look at her when she opened her mouth to speak, then snapped it shut again.

"Your mother is worried, my little bear." She turned her eyes toward him as he gazed off, thousands of yards away into nothing. She didn't dare say anything until she was told to, not even to apologize for worrying Ma. "You are behaving strangely, she says. I tell her you are growing up." Oh, so they had noticed. "Though I wish you would not."

No surprises there. Youngest of three and only girl, things had been different for her than for her brothers. She was and always had been Da's girl, having him wound about any finger she deigned to use, though her respect for him far exceeded any willingness to exploit that. She unscrewed the lid of the thermos, pouring out a measure of Ma's homemade hot chocolate before passing the rest off to Da.

"You are special." Despite her best efforts, she sighed, earning that *look* from Da, made all the more stern by the patterned tattoo that traveled up the side of his brown face and over his eye. He was not done, and it was not yet time for her commentary on the topic. "We've all known it, as any member of this family would treasure any other." Now she nodded knowing this included Innes, and probably someday whoever had the ill luck to follow one of her brothers home for a family dinner. "But even they do not know the full of it, so it is seldom something to talk about."

He sipped his hot chocolate, taking his time with his thoughts. No force in the world would hurry him when he did not wish to be hurried. As Kahrin was the wind of a storm, he was the rock. Or a strong tree which learned to bend but never break as the wind blew.

"My impatient daughter. She could not wait to get to town to be born." Kahrin rolled her eyes. Da loved telling the story of how she was literally born in a barn, thus prone to leaving doors open and exhibiting sometimes very uncouth behavior. As if anyone in the Quirke family was couth, hospital-born or otherwise. "Small and too soon, and very, very angry that her choice to come so quickly had consequences." Oh, he loved this part, too. How she squalled her head off in the cold until she could be swaddled in his flannel shirt. The story was so popular that Ma had turned that shirt into a stuffed bear which Kahrin still had in her room. "When I saw the fireball spirit in the woods that night, I feared you would be taken from us before you would live."

Okay, that part was new. "Fireball spirit?"

"Don't interrupt." He glanced at her, and when he believed she was suitably remorseful he took a long drink from the thermos and some quiet contemplation, then he continued. She curled her toes inside her boots, restless, and breathed deep and slow.

"*Cinkwun a'nak*." That did not tell her much, and Da allowed another long pause before he continued, as if directly defying her sometimes choleric nature. "They can be sent by a medicine man to lead evil to cause harm, or eliminate it." He looked at her directly now. "When your mother fell ill and you did not, I knew what you were."

Kahrin blinked. Several times. This conversation just turned weird in a way she'd never expected. "You knew?" She didn't have to clarify what it was he knew. "All this time? How?" She wanted to be angry at Da for keeping this from her, instead she felt relieved. Someone else *knew*. That he, in particular, knew comforted her beyond any expectation she could have dreamed.

She watched as Da bit the inside of his mouth. Hard. She stiffened, not understanding. He held up his hand, palm up, his eyes focused on something she could not see. He looked at her, then back at his hand and hopped down from the tailgate, taking several paces away from her. He swept his hand outward and tipped it over, pouring out something unseen. Until a spiral of green shot from the ground, bidden by whatever her father had done. Tiny and delicate, small white flowers bloomed, the petals shaped like droplets. Kahrin sucked air over her teeth. Her head shook back and forth, small motions at first, then larger, harder, shaking strands loose from her braid. "No. No, that's not real. I would have known!"

"How, *makoons*? How can you know what does not know you?" Da approached her once more, cradling her chin gently in his cupped hand and turning her eyes up to meet his. Aside from the slightly darker patch of brown in hers, they matched the hazel of her father's. "I know what you did to save the unicorn." He *knew* about Yelena? "I know the mark on Innes' face. You will both attract terrible things for different reasons."

Kahrin's mind spun, like Pickle chasing the stub of his own tail just now, never catching it but still trying. He let a woof as if to confirm her analogy.

Da's face turned very sad, giving a rare glimpse of his age. "Now that you are grown, I cannot protect you as I have, so you must guard yourself." Like a clue-by-four to the head, Da swung around to what he could have just said without all the to-do. "I do not know how to keep us safe if you disregard my protections."

"Protections? Protections from what?"

He grasped both of her hands now, his words swelling with earnestness that seemed unlike him. "Most like you do not survive infancy. I was meant to drown you as soon as I knew." He leaned forward and pressed his forehead to hers, letting them share breath between them. "I could not. You had a piece of my heart already, as you will forever. You are the greatest piece of me, one I will not let anyone take away."

"So, why tell me this, now?" She grasped her Da's face on either side, shaking and feeling the sting of wetness welling in her eyes.

"Because you need to be careful who you invite into your life." Was that not true of everyone? "You bring strange men into our home. You invite those we do not know." Finally he got to the point she should have known was coming. Something Evan Greves had hinted at. "Those with magic are threatened by that which would undo it." He sighed, his shoulders slumping under an invisible yoke. "You could have been a force of destruction, and could still be, one which I may pay for yet." There was a piece she was still missing. Some 'but' that he'd dodged until just now. "You have something none like you had before."

"Innes."

He nodded. "Separately you are at risk. Vulnerable to this world of things seen and unseen. By those who believe, and who do not." Somewhere, Innes was feeling righteous in his long-held faith. "Together, there is nothing stronger than what your friendship has forged."

The side of her mouth twitched upward. "You also protected Innes." Da nodded. "That's why you've always welcomed him."

"Innes is a True Believer, and the unicorn has marked him as such for the world of magic to see. It's meant to be a mark of honor, but he will be a prize for whoever catches him. He is your spear just as you are his shield.

Kahrin thought she understood. "And now that we're both grown up, and he's moved away..." she trailed off.

Da picked up the thought without her needing to finish. "I knew this time would come, but I was hoping it would not be this soon." He pressed a kiss to her brow.

Kahrin stared at their joined hands, her father anchoring her as it felt her whole life had flipped over. "So, you're not kicking me out, but it's time for me to go."

Da answered with only a single nod.

Kahrin impressed herself with how easily she was able

to take all of this in, even if she was sure the processing would take longer. It made sense, now that she had all the pieces.

There remained only one more thing to ask. "So why do you mess with Innes so much? Make him think you don't like him?"

Da shrugged, sliding back up onto the tailgate and opening the lunch box. "It amuses me."

CHAPTER EIGHTEEN

Innes

Innes pulled his pillow over his head. If he ignored her, she would go away. The problem with that was twofold: no she would not, and he did not want her to. What time did she get up to be here so early? What had possessed him to give her keys to his old car, enabling her to do exactly what she was doing right now?

His phone started ringing. Again. It vibrated to the edge of his nightstand before it stopped. It started ringing again almost immediately, this time tumbling to the floor. "You're not getting out of this so easily," he grumbled to the self-destructive phone as he threw his blankets back and rolled out of bed. He padded around the couch and circled to the door, leaning his head on it before undoing the chain and the bolt.

"Finally!" Kahrin grumbled as she came in, a bag under one arm and a car carrier of beverages in hand. At least she knew enough to feed him if she was going to knock on his door before even God was awake. "You know that green button on the phone screen answers a call? I thought you were dead! I was about to call the police."

"I was asleep. Like most reasonable people at this hour." He scrubbed his eyes with a fist. "How was I supposed to know you'd be here before the sun?" Tired though Innes was, he gave her a bleary-eyed smile. "Demanding to be let in. You're like an indoor-outdoor cat, you know that?"

"Which is why you should give me a key of my own." She made a fair point, even if he didn't want to admit it. If he gave her a key, she was more likely to come in and sleep rather than waking him up, settling for warming her icy feet against him as an alternative to antics. He watched her set her burden of pastries and beverages on the table before she spun on a foot and rushed him.

He let out an oof as her arms caught around his chest in a crushing hug. As if she hadn't just seen him a handful of days ago, and wouldn't see him the day after tomorrow. When he wrapped his arms about her, she was shaking, though she gave no other indication that anything was wrong. He dropped a kiss onto the crown of her head.

"Not that I'm unhappy to see you, but what's going on?" He rubbed her back, his groggy mind still trying to puzzle out why she was here. When he loosened his arms to pull back away from her she wrapped hers tighter, not yet ready to let him go.

"I needed you." Not needed to see or needed to talk to. He smiled affectionately into her hair. "Need. Want. Whatever. I love you."

"I love you, too." It hadn't always been so easy for her to say that, which was odd, given the way the Quirke family loved one another so openly, but she'd gotten there in her own time. It still warmed him every time he heard it, and he still made certain that she heard it back every time she bravely said it. "Kahrin, are you okay?"

She nodded against his chest, then stopped and shook her head in the same place. "I didn't know. There's so much

I didn't know, even though you always told me. I think I believed you, but I didn't want to. Or maybe I was jealous because it wasn't as easy for me to believe what I couldn't see."

Sometimes it took a little while to let Kahrin work through her convoluted line of thinking so he could catch up. Honestly, he was too tired this time and needed her to make sense. "Come on." He pulled her hoodie off one sleeve at a time, since she was unwilling to let go of him entirely, and tossed it aside. "Shoes," he ordered, shifting his weight first one way and then the other while she kicked them off. That left her in her running top and leggings, as if she'd decided mid-run to just get in the car and come here. Which was not outside the realm of possibility.

"Let's get in the bed," he coaxed.

"You'll fall asleep." She rested her chin in the divot of his sternum and looked up at him. Her big, pretty, mismatched eyes held onto something she wasn't telling him, but danced with her impatience to.

"That's the idea," he confessed. "But I promise not to until you're ready."

"Fine."

Taking his wins where he could, Innes stepped backward, dragging her with him a few paces before he just picked her up and carried her, like a hapless maiden, and got them both into the bed so he could curl around her.

"Do you remember," she started into his shoulder before she shuffled so she could speak unencumbered, "when Da would take us all camping?" How could he forget? Not only was Da Quirke terrifying, but he knew the woods far too well. Every time they went out Innes worried he might not return with the rest of them. Of course,

Brecken and Alec had helped put that idea into his head. "We would go for hikes, and Da told you not to let me get lost?"

"I believe he said either we both come back or I shouldn't bother." More or less. His fingers trailed down the length of her braid and pulled the elastic free so he could tease her hair loose and run his hand through it.

"Whatever." Oh, sure. *Now* she didn't care about semantics. "The point is that he meant for us to stay together, so we were safe."

"Oh, that was perfectly clear." He didn't know where she was going with this. "You liked to wander off. Well, that's not really a past-tense statement." While he wouldn't do anything as cliché as calling her a free spirit, Kahrin certainly followed her own path, even if she had to stomp down the vegetation to make one.

"It wasn't me he was worried about." Wait, what? Kahrin pulled back so she could see his face. Like she was studying it for a reaction. "Not just me. You, too."

"Kahrin, what are you talking about?" The braid finally unraveled, and he began the process of gently working the tangles out. "Did you drive all the way here just for this?"

"Yes. Because it all makes sense now. We're two halves of a whole." Even with all the conviction she put behind it, he had no idea what she meant. "He didn't mean getting lost in the woods, though that was probably part of it. He meant from one another."

"Kahrin," he started, only to be cut off as she pulled away and sat up, tailor style.

"Da's an Adept."

Wait, *what*? "An Adept? You mean like–"

"Just like Evan Greves. Only, I assume he's not evil."

She canted her head, looking off into the distance. "His concept of right and wrong seems a little iffy, but overall, not evil."

The drowsiness he'd been fighting cleared away. "So, your father...knows about you? About you being a Hole in the World?" Even as the words sounded odd, it made sense.

"He knows about all of it. Me. Yelena." Still, after all of this time, his chest squeezed to hear her name. "How Evan died. How I got hurt." His arms reached for her once more, unwilling to remember that horrifying moment he thought she'd died without feeling her warm and alive against him. She came to him easily. "And about you."

"What about me?"

"About that fancy unicorn's kiss, and how it will attract all sorts of evil to you." She beamed up at him. "It marks you. You're special. Your blood." She laid her hand over his chest, above his heart and made a face as if she'd never felt it before that moment. "Your soul."

He laughed, softly. "Far be it for me to doubt a fairy tale."

"It's not a fairy tale," she chided with affection. "Anyway, I think I should move out of my parents' house." He blinked. Not out of disapproval, but disbelief. As much as Kahrin claimed to hate being stuck there on the farm, he didn't believe she'd ever leave it for good. Not without a team of horses hitched up, and even then, he wouldn't be so hasty as to put money on the horses. "And move here."

"Here?" He didn't mean for his voice to pitch so high, but she'd caught him off guard.

"Not *here* here." No, this apartment was too small for the two of them. One of them would wind up stuffed in the garbage with a sock gagging their mouth. Maybe both, the way their luck went. "To this town. Closer to you." She shrugged her shoulders. "So we can be together." She rolled her eyes and gave him the obligatory, "I know, not like *that*." At this point it felt more like a verbal tick than anything else with as often as they said it. Neither of them needed reminding, but it was a habit as comfortable as a well-worn sweatshirt.

"You sound sure."

"I'm very sure. I've never been so sure."

"What about college?"

She shrugged in the circle of his arms. "I'll finish eventually. Just...not with a professor who's trying to get in my pants."

His temper flared, and she saw it on his face and winced. "I thought you were done with him."

"I don't know. Probably. Maybe."

"Maybe?"

She huffed. "Do you mind if we don't talk about that right now?"

He did. He wanted to know what André had done this time, when he shouldn't have had the opportunity to do anything, since they already knew he was an ass. But, he could tell she wouldn't give him anymore on it right now, not without a fight, and he did not want to argue. They knew to pick their battles. While Kahrin often chose all of them, he was more selective. "Okay." He took a deep breath and blew thoughts of André out his nose and hopefully far, far away from his bed. "So, when's the big move?"

"I don't know, yet. There's a lot to figure out and I don't know where to start." She chewed her lip, a pretty flush dusting her light brown cheeks. "Fortunately, I know someone who's already made a move to the big city."

"You do?" He grinned, even as she dug her fingers into his ribs to tickle him as punishment. "Who?" he almost managed before he choked off in laughter.

"A friend of mine." She squealed softly when he caught her hands and pinned them in place.

"A friend?"

"Best friend. He's ruggedly handsome. Devastating eyes. And he's like, one-third wiener."

Innes choked, a rumble of laughter starting in his chest. "That sounds like a lot to handle." He dipped his head and caught her up in a kiss, strangely not tired anymore.

"Maybe for a lesser woman," she murmured against his lips. "But I'm special." She bit his lower lip, sending a bolt of heat through him. "It's not so much to me."

Oh, now that was unnecessary. "You take that back."

"Make me?" She poked her tongue out at him, lifting her hips against his.

He shook his head. "That's not how this works." He didn't miss the snatch of breath she caught when his hands tightened on hers.

"Show me I'm wrong?"

"Better," he growled, his lips finding her neck and his teeth dragging over her skin until he nipped the lobe of her ear. "And I will."

CHAPTER NINETEEN

Innes

To say that Kahrin had not thought through her decision to move to the city beyond knowing she had to drive to tell Innes about it right away was an understatement. Naturally, she considered this the most important part. Not the minor details, like where she would live or how she would pay for it.

Fortunately, these were things in which Innes was experienced, having already moved to the city and navigated Kahrin's whirlwind mind. Life was funny like that.

They got a rather late start on the day, considering the time Kahrin had arrived. This being such an important decision for her, it felt more appropriate to celebrate than point out all the missing points of her plan (or lack thereof). Kahrin's excitement was infectious; it wasn't difficult to keep him awake, even in such a comfy bed.

Emboldened by the confidence of her new life choice, Kahrin made a suggestion as her lips traveled up the line of his throat which both surprised him and made his blood run hot. That it surprised her as much as it did him only made it more enticing, and not even because of the joining of bodies (though that was not necessarily a downside!). Rather, that she trusted him so thoroughly as she lay back, urging him to follow, and drawing his hands toward her throat. Her vulnerability was intoxicating beyond comprehension. They ventured into this new act with utmost care. Always gently, with what they both knew was risky, even dangerous behavior. Their mutual exploration of their respective and unexpectedly aligning proclivities had introduced some things which required delicacy. It meant slowing down from the heat of barreling hormones, reassuring one another of trust. It meant working out a nonverbal signal in case it got to be too much. It demanded a slow and steady buildup, one that frustrated both their patience, but the release was unlike anything he'd known. Afterward, an unexpected softness fell over Kahrin, presenting in a rush of emotions, and even soft crying. They dozed together in a tangle of limbs, where she insisted she felt safe, and the intimacy gave him a contentment unique to knowing he could provide that for her. Being needed in such a way played to his desire to be a protector, and that Kahrin of all people asked for it made it all the more precious.

While Kahrin showered Innes made a list of the various things they'd need to address, in the order of importance. This way they had an idea of where to start the preparations. It would also help to solidify her decision. While Innes would never unduly pressure her one way or the other on something as big as this, he knew his best friend. For as big as she liked to talk about not being afraid of anything and wanting to get out their tiny hometown, if left to her own, she'd talk herself out of it, even if she truly wished to follow through.

"It doesn't have to be a fancy job, Pretty Mouth," she insisted, thermos of orange juice in hand while they walked the sidewalks in the modest business district. "I'm not especially skilled at anything, unless there's a sudden demand for mucking pens here in the city. That means I'll be able to learn to do anything."

Already they'd noted a juice bar, a coffee house, a bookstore, and a bicycle repair shop, none of which required her to have any experience and little more than a plucky outlook.

"There's a few things to consider. Wages. Hours. Opportunity for advancement." He ticked each one on his fingers.

She took a long drink of juice. "Juice bar and bike shop. It's not hard."

"Those are both minimum-wage positions," he pointed out. Even as he knew he was making important points, he shook his head with affection, knowing he was wasting his breath.

"But, I like juice, and I like bikes." Such conviction! "How much different can it be, fixing a bike than fixing the tiller at home?"

"Do you want an answer to that?" He lifted an eyebrow as his stomach began gnawing at him. "Or should I just accept this is a done deal and suggest lunch?"

"The last one." She hopped a few strides to him, slipping an arm around his waist as they walked the distance back toward the apartment to get his car. "I can search for places to live on the computer at home and we can look at them next week." She shrugged, so casual about all of it. So sure of herself, here with him walking beside her. Innes hoped to give her enough support to ensure she was still confident in her choice when she went back to the farm.

Wasn't that what helped him adjust when he'd first moved? His voracious need to get away from the small town where everyone knew his family, his oh-so-tragic orphaned past, sure. Where they knew that Brodie didn't mind housing him, but wasn't shy about expressing the additional burden that was feeding and clothing him. If Kahrin and her family hadn't supported him, had he not met Emilia as he did in those first few weeks, would he be doing as well as he was now? He doubted it.

"After this weekend," he reminded her. A grin broke bright across his face. "I'm really looking forward to it. All weekend, uninterrupted, with my best friend."

"We don't even have to wear clothes if we don't want." He knew she meant due to the privacy of being all alone and so close, though in the aftermath of their morning, it evoked other ideas entirely. She must have sensed as much, adding, "I'd like to try that one thing again. Maybe actually push through it."

That sent an unexpected spike of heat through him as he regarded her. The memory of the feeling of her pulse thrumming beneath his fingers before she'd (understandably) lost her nerve, followed by his losing his nerve when they tried again. It was still fresh enough in his mind.

"It's the middle of January," he reminded her, getting back to the topic at hand. As if that was going to matter when they had a fire, a pile of blankets, and whatever books he decided to bring. She lifted an eyebrow, communicating some of what he was thinking as if she could read his thoughts. Before they could get distracted and sidetracked, he grabbed her hand to hurry their trip to the car.

"You know I could treat you to lunch for helping me,

right?" she reminded him while they walked away from the campus parking garage. Miraculously, it hadn't taken them long to snag a parking spot after their drive. Sometimes it took as long to find an empty stall as it did to drive there at all. "We don't have to eat in your cafeteria."

"I know, but if I don't use the meal money, then I lose it." That seemed to mollify her, and she put up no further argument about it. He pulled her along toward the eatery, in the door, and up the stairs.

About midway up, he pulled to a stop, remembering the last conversation they had about Evangeline, because there she stood at the top of the stairs, just outside the door to go in. He'd never seen her here before. "Promise to behave," he murmured into Kahrin's ear.

She lifted a brow, her smile affixed crookedly. "Do I normally not?" That was a loaded question, and he didn't have time to give her the bawdy answer it deserved. Her eyes landed on Evangeline as the young woman waved to them. Well, to him. "Oh," was all Kahrin said, though to her credit she didn't resist their continuing up.

"Innes!" Evangeline's voice rose up in greeting, ringing out like a bell in a sharp contrast to when he'd seen her at the store. They'd not spoken since then. "I didn't expect to see you here." She tilted her head, her pale ginger-blonde hair swaying in wide ringlets. She swung a knee back and forth, making the fabric of her loose, wide-legged trousers swish.

Something tugged at the corners of his mind. Something warm and welcoming and just out of his reach. He was being beckoned by something he couldn't see or hear. He dismissed it. "We're just getting a quick lunch."

Though it was impossible for Evangeline to have

missed her, she looked at Kahrin as if seeing her for the first time. "Oh." Her smile widened as she backed up a stair. "Nice to see you again."

"I'm sure." Kahrin tightened her grip on Innes' hand.

Sometimes, just before a storm, the world went very still. Somewhere off in the distance a bird chattered happily on its perch, blissfully unaware of whatever standoff was going on between Evangeline and Kahrin right now. The fine hairs on Innes' neck stood the same as if the air hung heavy with unreleased lightning.

"I didn't expect to see you so soon before your big trip this weekend. How long is she staying?" Evangeline's eyes met Innes', as if Kahrin was not standing right there to answer for herself. "I was hoping we could make good on that rain check."

Innes put his arm around Kahrin's shoulders, squeezing her tight against him. Every muscle he could feel in her was taut, same as if she were about to start a run or reach her release. "Kahrin's going to move here."

Evangeline's gaze shot to Kahrin, eyes wide even as her face lit up. "That's wonderful!"

He could feel that odd pull at him once more. Something which wanted him to lean closer to Evangeline. To inhale that scent of sugar and taste that utter sweetness on her tongue again. Yet, there was a calm void beside him. Not even calm. Calm would have been something, and this was nothing. Nothing but Kahrin and her hand in his. But it felt safe. Safe from what? That made no sense.

"Well, we won't keep you," Kahrin chirruped, urging him to follow her the rest of the way into the cafeteria. The odd tugging was gone.

He waved his fingers in farewell, somewhat abashed,

but Evangeline spun around. "I'd love to join you."

Innes looked at Kahrin and back to Evangeline. "I don't see why not."

That was the wrong answer, evident in the tightening of Kahrin's jaw, but whatever the reasoning for disapproval, she kept it to herself. The trio went inside, Innes using his meal card to pay for himself and Kahrin. Maybe the food wasn't great, being mass produced and meant to be filling more than anything else, but there it was. Kahrin didn't seem to mind, and he was used to it by now. Evangeline picked at her food, doing little else with it.

"I've never been up to the lake." Evangeline leaned her chin on a hand, her lashes fluttering around her pretty golden-brown eyes.

"You should go sometime." Kahrin popped a limp fry into her mouth and chewed it with a grin on her face. "We've been going with my family since we were kids."

He couldn't put a finger on it, but there was something challenging in Kahrin's voice. If he didn't know better, he'd have sworn it was jealousy. He did know better, and that meant something was wrong. Innes pushed his chair back and stood. "We should get going. We're heading up tonight." Sort of. They'd pass through the Quirke farm first, for the night so he could give Ma and Da Quirke his assurances that they'd be safe. And probably stay for moose pot pie made with Ma's homemade crust, if he had to guess.

Kahrin's phone buzzed, and Innes looked up in time to see her silence it without answering. "André."

She didn't need to say any more.

"He's not invited." Well, of course not. Kahrin hopped up to her feet, clapping her hands together. "So, we'll see you around."

"Would you," Evangeline shook her head, waving a hand about instead of finishing her thought. "No, it's silly. Never mind."

"What?" Innes asked her, collecting his tray with Kahrin's to take care of. He gave her a smile to encourage her to continue.

"Would you mind if I came up? Maybe Sunday?"

He looked to Kahrin. She wasn't going to like it if he said yes. He could see it in her eyes. "I...um." He swallowed, unsure how to proceed here. It wasn't so much that he minded her inviting herself, though that was very abrupt, just that she didn't seem to get the importance of the trip. "See, we have this whole thing planned."

"Say no more." That disappointment crossed Evangeline's face again, though she tried to hide it. "I wouldn't dare intrude." She stood and followed them, grabbing Innes' arm, stopping him just before the door. "A moment?" Her eyes fluttered closed as she turned her head down, her lips moving as if she were trying to think of something to say.

"I'll catch up," he told Kahrin, tossing her the keys to his car so she could wait in it. She hesitated, looking doubtful, then nodded. As she stepped through the door, a man shoved past them, knocking into Kahrin and sending her spilling down the concrete stairs with a shriek.

CHAPTER TWENTY

Kahrin

There was something wrong about Evangeline, and it wasn't just that she was kind of a pushy jerk. Kahrin couldn't quite figure out what, and she had the sinking suspicion that it was of the *she couldn't see it* variety. Something about the way she fluttered her eyes at Innes felt like the woman was holding a knife to his throat.

What Kahrin did know beyond doubt was they needed to get out of this cafeteria. Before Evangeline got any ideas. "So, we'll see you around," Kahrin said pleasantly—too pleasantly—as she hopped up from her seat.

"Would you," Oh no. They needed to go. Now. "No, it's silly. Never mind."

"What?" Dammit, Innes, and damn his manners. He busied himself gathering up their trays so Kahrin couldn't grab him by the arm and drag him out the door. Even though she knew she had to. She just *knew*.

"Would you mind if I came up? Maybe Sunday?"

Kahrin met Innes' eyes, silently begging him to make an excuse, any excuse at all, why that was not possible. Assuming that pointing out how Kahrin did not want her there would not be sufficient. "I...um. See, we have this whole thing planned."

Yeah. A whole thing. It would be hard to not wear pants

and explore darker kinky urges and curiosities with someone else in the room. Not that it was the point of their trip, but it was a part, and one she was looking forward to. Innes was the only person she could trust as she figured out these things she was learning about herself. More to the point, she didn't trust this woman to not be planning to smother or stab them in their sleep. After all, not every murderer needed a supernatural reason to kill the object of their affections.

"Say no more," Evangeline said with a wave of her hand that absently brushed against the arm of someone behind her. Oh, she was good. That pout on her stupid pretty lips and that unbelievable attempt to look like she was trying not to look sad. "I wouldn't dare intrude."

That was good enough for Kahrin, and she grabbed Innes' hand as she walked toward the door, only for him to stop suddenly, his fingers losing contact with hers.

Kahrin turned to see what was holding him up. Literally. Evangeline had him by the arm. He looked to Kahrin, then tossed his keys in a clean arch so she could snatch them out of the air. "I'll catch up."

Oh, sure. She opened her mouth to argue, and maybe that was why she didn't see the man pushing past people, until he came straight at her. His eyes focused on her, though it was like he didn't see her, the way he strode toward her. She had time to dodge, and he adjusted, intent to collide with her, and likely also intending for her to go careening down the stairs. Which she did.

Kahrin shrieked out, barely remembering to duck her head. She saw her legs fly over her vision. Everything spun about, and she couldn't even make sense of the commotion. Not until she came to a stop at the bottom. Face up, feet above her on the stairs. She couldn't tell just yet if anything was hurt. She was just grateful to be conscious. And alive. That was a lot of stairs.

"Kahrin!" Innes caught up to her, racing on his toes down the steps. "Kahrin, are you okay?"

Was she? She was still taking inventory when the man who'd knocked her down hurried his way over to them. Innes, after fussing and making sure that moving wouldn't kill her, helped her up, supporting her as she waited for the world to stop spinning about. Her eyes focused on the man, who looked confused. Like he'd just shaken free from a daze of his own.

Innes curled around her protectively. "You need to watch where you're going!" he snapped. "You could have killed her."

"I didn't..." The man blinked like he was dazzled by the snow, his breathing erratic. He took a step back, appearing worried Innes might hit him. If he could have done it without letting go of her it would not have been outside the realm of possibility. "I don't know what happened. I wasn't even ready to leave."

Words tumbled back and forth between Innes and her apparent assailant, but Kahrin didn't notice. She leaned her head against Innes' chest for balance, though she felt like she was being a tad theatrical. She'd survived a car wreck, a concussion, a rebound concussion and stabbing herself. A spill down the stairs was no big deal. Her eyes scanned around the area, finally meeting Evangeline's gaze at the top. Evangeline's pink lips pulled in a thin line, her expression cold. Kahrin could have sworn she saw a haze of smoke rising from her. That had to have been her banged up head.

No. No it didn't have to be that. Because this wasn't the first time odd things happened that Kahrin couldn't explain. Was Evangeline trying to kill her? That made no sense. Unless...

"Hey, Innes, can we just go home?" She shook her head, feeling a wash of dizziness come over her. She swallowed hard, hoping to keep the soggy fries from making an encore. "Your apartment, I mean."

"Of course." His muscles twitched with tension. Even if she wasn't feeling shaky, getting him out of this situation seemed a good idea.

It took Evangeline more time to get to the bottom. Had Kahrin noticed her limp before? "Are you all right?" Kahrin might have believed she was actually concerned if she'd been looking at her when she said it. Her golden eyes narrowed, then shifted to the man next to them, and finally to Innes.

"I'll be fine," she assured her. Just in case she actually did care. "I've survived worse."

"Well, that's a relief." Evangeline rested a hand on Innes' arm. "I'll stop by later to see how she's doing?"

"No." Kahrin had not meant to say it out loud, and yet it popped out all the same. "No. Just leave us alone."

"Kahrin." Innes' voice cut sharp, but his eyes were full of concern. The intensity in her look must have tipped him off that something was amiss. He didn't argue further. Instead, he kissed the top of her head. "I'll talk to you later," he called over his shoulder to Evangeline as he led Kahrin to the car at the pace of her choosing. Which was much faster than her eyes and stomach wanted it to be.

"Kahrin, what's going on?" he asked as soon as they were in and buckled. "Are you hurt?"

"I'll probably have some aches and pains later, but I don't mind." She let her head rest against the seat as his almost silent car started moving. Having more than a little experience in hitting her head, she closed her eyes to avoid the dizziness. She breathed out, quietly praying to get through what she had to say without starting a fight. "I think Evangeline did it."

"What?" To his credit, Innes didn't slam on the breaks in his shock. "What are you talking about? She wasn't anywhere near you."

"I know. Did you see the guy who knocked me over? He didn't know what happened any more than I did. I don't think he did it of his own will."

"Okay. Explain?"

"Magic." Kahrin took a deep breath and blew it out, her cheeks puffing. "Not like Evan, though." When he didn't answer right away, she bit the inside of her mouth, trying to decide the best way to approach this. "Do you trust me?"

He glanced her way before he changed lanes. "You know I do. With my life and more."

"Okay. And you know I trust you the same. And I'd never do anything to intentionally hurt you."

"Kahrin, what is it?" An edge touched his voice, that little thread of worry she couldn't get him to abandon even if she wanted to. Which she did not. Right now his tendency to worry over her was her ally.

"Evan had to cut himself to use magic." Her teeth sank into the flesh of her lip before she added, "Just like my Da."

Innes' face scrunched in thought, as if he'd forgotten that information.

"I don't think she's human."

He was quiet the space of a few heartbeats, letting a

popcorn chuckle. "Kahrin, that's quite a leap."

She couldn't tell yet if she needed to be offended or not. "I think she's using magic, and she's not letting blood to do it. If she's using life force, it's not her own."

His humor dimmed. "So, what do you think she is?"

"I don't know. This is your area of expertise, not mine."

To her relief, he nodded, taking that in and giving this the seriousness she believed it deserved. "And you're making this guess based on what, exactly?"

"Well, she hates me, for one. Probably for the same reason Evan was wary of me. And I think she made that guy push me down the stairs to get me out of her way."

"Your proof is that someone knocked you over without seeing you," he gave her a side glance as if she did not know she was five feet and one single inch tall, out of the usual lower periphery of people around her, "and that a girl who's interested in me is jealous of you?"

"Yes."

"I don't know. We can't just go around accusing people of being—"

"Unicorns?"

Maybe that was a low blow, but it had the desired effect. "Come on. That was different."

"Yeah, because you just knew and I trusted you, even though I had no way to know you were right." She couldn't see or sense the magic, but that was hardly the point, was it? He couldn't argue with that, and to his credit, didn't try. "So, I'm invoking unicorn."

"You're invoking unicorn?" He turned into the lot behind his building, not saying anything else until he was helping her out of her side of the car. Her hips and shoulders were starting to ache and she didn't fight when he insisted she lean upon him as they climbed the stairs back up to his apartment. "So, what does that mean?"

"Well? When you thought Yelena was a unicorn, I trusted you, even if I didn't believe you." Again, because she couldn't see all the magic that was going on around them. That didn't apply here. "I believed in you."

Once inside, he helped her shed her shoes and pants, helping her get comfortable, even indulging her demand for her favorite borrowed sleep shirt, and no, he couldn't just give it to her, because then it wouldn't be her favorite borrowed sleep shirt. André called twice more, and twice more she sent him to voicemail. Hopefully he would get the message.

"So, you want me to believe you, that Evangeline isn't human." She nodded. In her mind it really was that simple. "And, what? That she's trying to kill you?"

She shook her head. "No." He lifted his brows. "I think she's trying to kill you."

CHAPTER TWENTY-ONE

Kahrin

Several things caught Kahrin's attention at once: first and strangest was the smartcar parked in Innes' spot next to the goat pen; next was the lack of Pickle running out to greet her as she pulled in; then she looked at the farmhouse, where her parents were watching out the kitchen window. Her teeth ground together as she parked the little K-car in front of the barn. Aggravated as she was, she hopped out of the car without turning it off, leaving the door open so a very timely Taylor Swift song blared as she stomped over to see stupid André's stupid face in his stupid smartcar.

"What are you doing here?" she shouted, smacking her hand against the driver's side window. "You can't be here." This was exactly why she never let dates pick her up at home, on account of their then knowing where home was.

André held up a hand as he started opening the door. He looked terrible, his curls flattened and frizzy, and his eyes rimmed with red and bloodshot. Had he slept in his car overnight? There was no way Da and Ma would have allowed that. "You weren't at school today."

"Who are you? My truant officer?" She threw her hands out to her sides. "Because you're not my boyfriend, so where I am and when is none of your business."

BLOOD OF THE TRUE BELIEVER

He stood, pushing his way out of the car. "Look, I wanted to give you a chance to explain." *Wait what?* "And I thought I could meet your parents and apologize."

"No." She held up one finger. "No, you are not meeting my parents. I already told them what happened—"

"What did happen?" he asked. Was he serious? "Because I still don't know, and we can't talk about it if you avoid me."

"Talk about what, André? You want to give me some more class notes? Don't bother. I'm dropping your stupid class and leaving the college."

The one thing that wasn't missing from this totally romantic moment was Innes—weirdly far behind her on the road—pulling in. He had the same reaction to his spot being taken as she had, veering at the last moment to park behind Kahrin's car. He got out of his car just in time to hear André's great answer.

"I want to talk about us."

It felt like something burst in her head. When she first opened her mouth to retort, a dry scoff was all that came. After sputtering her disbelief, she burst out into laughter. "You know, I've had a concussion *and* a second impact concussion. I once lost so much blood I was delirious, and that is the most nonsense thing I've ever heard." She waved her hands in front of her in his direction, like she was clearing away fog, because surely his brain was full of it. "There is no us!"

"Kahrin," Innes shut off his car as he called to her on the way to shutting off her car. A moment later he came up beside her. His brows drew tight in the middle, a single chunk of his silver hair dipping over his forehead. He pressed her keys into her hand. "Is everything okay?"

"Who's this?" André lifted a hand in Innes' direction.

Kahrin blinked, not understanding the question. Who's this? "That's Innes." Obviously.

That did nothing for André's attitude. "You mean the bed guy?"

Innes blanched. "What?"

Oh, sure. Great. She spun on a toe and looked at Innes. "We were fooling around on the trundle, and I—"

Innes pressed his lips together, and Kahrin was grateful for that streak of protectiveness over his privacy. He wouldn't raise the sort of fuss André was. That didn't mean there was nothing to say on the subject. "I sleep there."

"I know, which is why I changed my mind. That's your bed and I can't do that." She bit back *without you*, since it would do nothing to help anything, and would only serve to embarrass Innes. "So, he went out the window, and I washed the sheets. It's fine."

"Do you hear yourself?" André asked, his voice rising to a pitch. "How was any of that okay? I jumped out a second story window in my bare feet with no shirt."

"Yeah." She gestured to him, indicating how nothing was broken and he was in fact still alive. "And you're fine"

"You're acting like a child." He ran a hand over his face.

Kahrin blinked, and the laugh she let this time held no mirth. "You need to leave. If my Da comes out here, he won't be as nice as me." Maybe he'd set him on fire with his mind, which was probably a thing he could do. Well, she hoped not, but it was fun to think about.

"Come on. I'm cold." Innes grasped her elbow and urged her toward the house.

"Oh, sure. Go hide behind your parents." André huffed, tromping back toward his car. Halfway there, he spun back around and caught her by the wrist. "No, you know what? We're going to talk about this like adults."

She jerked her arm back, but his grip held fast. "Get your hands off me!"

"Okay, now," Innes started calmly, though his voice took on a hard edge she knew too well. Innes did not often lose his temper. "Let's all calm down."

"I really need some chili fries," she whined beneath her breath and bounced on her heels.

"This doesn't concern you," André spat, oblivious to her nonsense interjection. His grip tightened and Kahrin let out a small whimper. It didn't even hurt as much as it annoyed her. "Or maybe it does. I don't know."

"What does that mean?" Kahrin demanded. She stopped pulling away, looking up at André with an expectation that he answer her, and do it soon.

"I think you know what it means." He gestured with a jerk of his lips toward Innes, whose jaw tightened in response.

With a final twist that shot pain up to her shoulder, Kahrin finally wrenched her arm out of his grip and stepped back. "Innes is my best friend."

"Who has a bed in your room no one can sleep on." Um, yeah? So? "Look, I don't care if you like sleeping around, just tell me so I know if I'm going to get any."

"Two seconds ago you called me a child," she reminded him. "You can't have it both ways." She scrubbed her face with her hands. "Actually, you can't have any of it at all."

"I don't want to waste any more of my time. We need to talk."

"Wasting your time?" She shook her head, ready to tell him in graphic detail what he could do with his time, but she never got the chance.

Innes' fist connected with André's face so fast she would have missed it had she been able to blink. She shrieked. André swore into his cupped hands, blood already dripping between his fingers. Innes hopped back, shaking his hand out. She'd never doubted he could throw a punch, but she never thought she'd see it.

"What the hell?" André's voice came out choked and nasally as droplets of his blood stained the tread-upon snow.

So sure that he'd try to hit Innes back, Kahrin threw herself between them, her back to Innes' chest, and when André stepped in as if he was going to throw a strike of his own, she stood up straight. Fortunately, for André, he stopped himself, for only a handful of thrumming heartbeats later, Da's hand planted in André's chest and carefully, but firmly, pushed him back.

"You need to leave." Da's face darkened. Though André had several inches on him, Da's presence was much larger than the other man could ever hope for. "Kahrin," he spoke evenly over his shoulder, "take Innes inside and get him ice for his hand."

"Da?"

"I said go. Now." She hesitated, suddenly worried what might happen if she left her Da alone with André, but didn't resist when Innes tugged at her arm and drew her back. Surely Da wouldn't do anything rash? Though, upon further reflection, she decided that André had signed his own death warrant when he showed up here. She and Innes were all the way to the deck stairs when Innes' head whipped around in response to nothing Kahrin could see or hear. His dark eyes went very wide as he looked back at

Da and André.

"What?" she asked. She knew the answer, even if Innes never said it. It was what she couldn't see, couldn't feel, that answered her question. She looked over her shoulder as Innes led her up the stairs to the sight of André, his eyes unfocused but his manner much calmer, nodding. He got back into his car without a fight. That's when Kahrin took the lead and pulled the door open to get herself and Innes into the mudroom.

Inside, Ma stood at the dining table with a pile of laundry, folding it as she hummed, acting oblivious to everything going on outside. She held a dish towel out to the pair when they walked by, which Kahrin collected en route to the kitchen. So, Ma did know what was going on, or at least enough to be concerned. "I hope you two are hungry."

Kahrin was not.

She dragged Innes into the kitchen without answering. "Sit," she hissed, tromping immediately to the freezer and dispensing a good amount of ice into the towel. She hastily knotted it, peeked into the dining room, then brought the wrapped ice to the breakfast nook. "What did you see?" she asked, tone hushed as she leaned close to him so their words might pass to only one another. "I know you saw something."

"I'm not sure." He spread the towel around so the ice covered as many of his knuckles as possible. "Some kind of...glow, I guess. And there was this charge through the air."

"Magic." She didn't think she needed to spell it out for him. He was always the one who believed in these things. Some part of her was oddly jealous. She kept her voice low, suspecting that Ma did not know the full of it. And if she did not, Da had a reason for it. "You can see my Da doing magic."

He nodded, a look on his face explaining that even though he knew Da was an Adept, he wasn't prepared for actually seeing his magic in action.

"You shouldn't have done that," she added, lying her head on his shoulder, which was the universal signal of 'thank you for doing that really dumb thing you should not have done'.

"He shouldn't talk to you like that." He lifted the towel and peeked under it. "I don't think this is bad, actually. It probably won't swell."

"I hope not." To try and lighten the mood she added, "I kind of like those fingers, specifically." Her levity didn't take, and she frowned down at the table. "I'm sorry."

"Why are you sorry?" Innes grasped her chin to encourage her to look at him. "André was out of line."

"I could have hit him myself, you know." She rolled her eyes.

The corner of Innes' mouth twitched. "I wanted to save him some dignity."

She snorted a laugh, despite herself, and took a breath to calm. After a moment of quiet she clicked her tongue in consideration of her next words, then spit them out before she could change her mind. "Do you think I'm slutty?" she asked, her stomach knotting as she feared the answer.

"What?" He shook his head no. "Why would you even ask that?"

"Well, I mean, he's not wrong." She lifted and dropped her shoulders, sure Innes did not need her to explain which 'he' she meant.

Innes turned to look her square on. "There's nothing wrong with seeking out and satisfying your desires." That sounded so wise, even from him. "You enjoy the things you enjoy, and you enjoy them with people you trust who are willing to share them with you."

She glanced up, trying for a smile, and failing. She gave up and let a sigh, her cheeks and lips puffing. "I guess. It's just good that he doesn't know. You know?"

"Know what?" Innes tilted his head, raising an eyebrow in question.

"About my...weird things." It was obvious on his face that he didn't understand what she meant and she grunted her frustration. "You know." She shrugged again, her discomfort plain. "The weird things I like you to do to me. The hurting stuff."

He frowned again, but this time wrapped an arm around her and pulled her close. "There's nothing weird about you." He poked her in the rib, making her squirm as she tilted her head back to see his face. "Well, there's nothing weird about the things you like, anyway."

She rolled her eyes. "Ha, ha."

"I mean it." He sat back once more, his big bistre eyes on her. "I enjoy those things we're exploring together."

"Oh." That should have made her feel better. She wanted it to make her feel better because those were all very good things. "Well, that's good."

He pecked a kiss to the corner of her mouth. "When we get back from the lake, I want you to meet Emilia." He looked unsure about that, but she saw a definite resolve in his eyes. "I think you'd really like her."

"What? Like Evangeline?"

"No. Not like Evangeline at all." He smiled, tenderness

in his expression. "She helped me to...well she helps me figure out a lot of things. You two should just...talk. Maybe she could help you." He preempted her lifted eyebrow. "Help you not feel at odds about what you enjoy."

"O-kay." An uneasiness settled itself into her stomach. She didn't know how talking to someone who she could only assume was a bed partner of Innes' would help her. That ugly little knot of jealousy tightened her stomach once more, and she scolded herself. If he thought it would be good for her, she would try talking to whoever the mysterious Emilia woman was, with her generosity and adoration toward Innes. Because Kahrin trusted him, without hesitation. "When we get back, then."

"But!" he said, stealing another kiss, "in order to come back, we have to go at all, hm?"

She granted him another roll of her eyes, but this time she grinned as the knots in her belly relaxed. "Tonight, or in the morning?"

"Kahrin!" Da's voice boomed from the mudroom. "I would like to speak with you." She heard him stomping off his boots, and the storm door closing, smacking itself into place behind him. "And Innes, as well."

She winced, looking at Innes with an abashed look on her face. "Sounds like we're going in the morning." If at all.

CHAPTER TWENTY-TWO

Innes

Innes watched as Kahrin's Da wrote out a list in his slow scrawl, asking her Ma to see about picking up the items so they would have them in the morning. Personally, Innes didn't see the necessity, until he realized what it was: an excuse to get a little privacy with the two of them.

So, Ma Quirke did not know.

Once Ma assured they would all be sufficiently fed—as if not a single one of them ever had to fend for themselves—she happily went on her way, taking her knot of reusable grocery bags with her. Da helped her get the cooler into the truck, then returned to the dining room where the pair waited for his arrival.

The familiar foreboding Da Quirke always caused settled in Innes' stomach, but this time he was mostly sure it wasn't anything he'd done wrong. Mostly.

Da stood, a tactic Kahrin used many times to compensate for her diminutive stature. Arms crossed over his chest, he regarded both of them with green-and-brown hazel eyes that matched his daughter's, save for the little extra patch of brown in one of hers. For the first time Innes could remember, he saw what he was sure was fear on Da's face.

"Who knows your plans for the weekend?"

Innes looked at Kahrin, her large doll-eyes widening. They'd not considered keeping it quiet, because it was just a normal part of their lives that they would spend this kind of time together. Innes turned back and lifted his eyes to Da's. "Just some friends. People I know up in the city."

Da took this in, mulling it over like he was swishing a fine wine over every part of his tongue to take in all the subtleties of flavor. "*Makoons*?"

Kahrin stammered. "I didn't..." She stopped herself, her face sliding into a frown of worry. Innes reached over and grasped her hand, hoping to offer her comfort in whatever form he could for whatever it was troubling her. "I might have mentioned it on my date. I really don't remember."

Da Quirke nodded his head slowly. So slowly. He rubbed at the tattoo running over his eye, but didn't so much as make an audible sigh.

"Da? What's wrong?"

"I don't know yet." He looked between them. "Empty your pockets onto the table. Both of you."

Never in his years had Innes ever so much as considered disobeying Da Quirke when he gave an order of any type. He stood, methodically starting at the breast pocket of his flannel shirt and lying each item neatly in front of him. The blue handkerchief from Emilia, his keys, his wallet, and a receipt from the gas station where Kahrin had bought gas.

Kahrin was not so tidy. Items spilled onto the table in front of her. A gum wrapper, another gum wrapper, the rest of the pack of gum, her keys, an elastic band for her hair. Innes chuckled as she dumped a handful of receipts mixed with dollar bills, and she just shrugged.

Without touching anything Da studied their collective

rubbish and belongings, making no sound, only the motion of his chest giving any indication he'd not turned to stone. Innes wasn't being accused of anything, and still felt his armpits moisten. What was Da Quirke looking for? He didn't make them wait long to find out.

"Innes," he boomed. Innes flinched, some of the high points of his life flitting before his eyes. "Where did you get that?" He pointed to but did not touch the hanky.

He blinked. What did it matter? It was a little game of Emilia's. Still, he'd never mouthed off to Da Quirke, and he wasn't about to start now. "From a friend, sir."

Da grunted. "You have a very good friend. Powerful." Da leaned his weight on one brown, tattooed arm, balancing on his flattened palm. "A friend who worries about you."

"I don't understand."

Something passed between Kahrin and her father, one nearly imperceptible nod exchanged for another. Had Innes not seen them communicate like this hundreds of times, he might have missed it now. "It's a charm, and a very strong one." *Wait, what?* "Guard it as it guards you."

"Da, what's going on?" Kahrin asked, her voice very tiny in a way Innes did not like hearing.

"That..." Da's teeth clenched, the next word was forced through his lips, and pointed in the direction of the kitchen window, "man is bewitched."

"What?" Their voices overlapped.

"How is that even possible?" Kahrin's hands shot out wide at her sides. "If I'm this great Hole in the World, shouldn't that stop any magic he's using?" A very good question, the answer to which Innes was also interested.

Da Quirke shook his head. "I don't know, my little one.

It's been..." He wiped a hand over his hair, cut into a clean style that always looked slightly at odds with the rest of him. "What I know has been enough so far. That may no longer be the case. Charms aren't strictly magic. You don't have to be an Adept to make them work."

Kahrin's father looked distressed, which Innes was not used to seeing. Apparently Kahrin wasn't, either, as she dropped into her chair, mouth gaping.

"What can we do?" Innes asked the obvious question. "Cancel our plans? Call the police?" Kahrin shot him a *look*, as if she had any better idea what you did with bewitched maybe-stalkers.

Da answered, "Shower." Kahrin stood and Da fixed Innes with a stone gaze. "Separately. You'll have time for young foolishness later." Innes' face flushed hot. "Take your clothes off and put them straight into a trash bag. I will take care of them."

"Take care of them, how?" Kahrin demanded.

"Let's say it's good you emptied your pockets."

She didn't like that, and huffed. Innes nudged her, hopefully reminding her that while her favorite strappy running bra could be replaced, neither of them could be.

"Is there anything else I need to know before I let you two go off alone to the lake?"

"Nope!" Kahrin chirruped. She jumped from her chair. "I'll shower first, then."

"Oh, come on. Let me have a little hot water!" It was not the most manly of whining, but neither would be the shriek he'd let when hit with a freezing shower.

"I'll be quick. Bring the bag with you, please?" She started up the stairs, bouncing on each step on the balls of her toes. Innes started to round the table to do as she'd asked.

"Just a moment, son." Knowing everything he knew now, he wasn't sure that 'son' was as menacing as he'd always thought it was. "What are you not telling me?"

Oh, so many things. So, so many things that he was not going to share with his best friend's father when her father knew very well that they sometimes indulged in physical activities together.

"This friend of yours? You trust her?"

"Without a doubt," Innes answered automatically. If there was anyone he trusted close to how he trusted Kahrin, it was Emilia.

"She's left you a powerful protection charm. The question is: Why?"

"I don't..." Kahrin's worries regarding Evangeline came back to him very quickly, stinging as fresh as pressing a finger against an angry bruise. "There's this girl." Da raised his tattooed brow. "A woman. She likes me but...she wants things I can't give right now."

"Such a terrible burden, being handsome," Da replied with a droll twist of his lips. Right there is where Innes would have added a little 'hm?', and he could almost hear it.

"For some, I guess. Sir." Da snort-laughed, breaking the tension for just a heartbeat before his face hardened once more. What *else* was Innes leaving out? He swallowed. "Kahrin thinks she's trying to kill me."

"You might have led with that." Did he know how he looked when his face did that thing it was doing now? Surely he must, given how deftly he did it.

"I didn't think Kahrin was right, but since it was her Evangeline...well Evangeline didn't hurt her. Kahrin thinks she tried." This was not helping Da's mood, and within a matter of moments, Innes was explaining the incident in the cafeteria. "She's fine; I checked."

"You are not a doctor yet, Innes."

Innes swallowed and nodded. "Yes, sir. I mean, no, sir. I'll keep an eye on her. Sir."

"Yes. You will." Da made a thoughtful grunt in the back of his throat. "Things which seem coincidental seldom are. Do you think it's possible the charm and the girl are related?"

It added up, except for the part where Emilia knew he had a need of such a charm. "I suppose anything is possible, sir."

"Indeed. Truer words than I was ready for." Then, Da Quirke did the strangest thing which Innes had ever witnessed him do in the many, many years the Quirkes had welcomed him into their home. He rounded the large table and pulled Innes into a rib-cracking embrace. "And you will let *makoons* keep an eye on you."

He didn't know what to do. Oh, he knew how to hug, but he didn't know how to hug this man, right here. Only, it also didn't seem wrong, and for just the space of a breath, he buried his face into Da's shoulder, allowing a safe sensation to wash over him. "Thank you."

Da Quirke stepped back, his hands flat on the balls of Innes' shoulders, looking slightly up to him. "No unicorn would leave her mark on just anyone, and I would not trust anyone less worthy with what I love most. Remember that."

"Hey! Pretty Mouth!" Kahrin called from just out of sight, up the stairs. "Are you bringing that bag or not?"

Da lifted a hand in question, urging him to move faster.

"Believe me when I say you should not keep a Quirke woman waiting."

Innes chuckled into a cough and cleared his throat. "Of all the things I need to learn, you think that's one?" Da's eyes narrowed, though Innes could swear his lips twitched. "Right! I'm going."

CHAPTER TWENTY-THREE

Innes

"No, Pickle, you can't go with us." Innes tried his best to sound stern, which became difficult when trying to swallow down his laughter as the Quirkes' dog vied for attention. As if he lacked it!

For his part, Pickle rolled onto his back in the spot Innes set aside for the cooler Ma and Da Quirke had loaned him. Being that it was already a small car, the blue bully wasn't leaving much room for anything else. He woofed, doing his best to be reassuring that there was plenty of room for him to accompany them.

With a little more coaxing, and more than one bribe in the form of treats, Pickle abandoned the car in time for Kahrin to bring their things to the trunk—freshly washed, folded, and packed at Da's request—and hefted them into the hatch.

She shuffled them back into the allotted space and hopped to sitting on the edge. She swung her feet, her mismatched hazel eyes turning up to meet his, a slight crease of worry despite her best efforts to heed Da's wishes to not alert Ma to what was happening. "Are you sure you still want to go?" Even then, he could tell from the way she bit her lower lip, tugging it over her teeth, that she wanted the answer to be yes even if she knew it should be no.

Fortunately, or unfortunately depending on who was asked, Innes also wanted the answer to be yes, and nodded his head. He dipped forward, pecking her on the brow. "You heard your Da. We'd be no safer here, since we know whoever is after us knows where you live." Possibly, with all that had happened over the past days, they needed to get away more than ever. "Besides," he added with a twitch of his lips, "I believe a challenge was extended."

She blushed, a pretty dusting of pink across her light-brown face. There was no shame or embarrassment between them, but it was adorable all the same when she got flustered. "I'm going to last longer than you." Her chin took on that defiant lift she pulled off so well. "And if I do, the real challenge will be you making good on your end of the bet." Her brow twitched upward. "Or do you think the cold is too much of an obstacle."

Innes growled, letting a small laugh as he leaned closer to her ear. These new games they played were different, different even from Emilia's, but intriguing in a way that made them almost irresistible. And if you couldn't explore that with your best friend, then who? "I'm sure you'll help me out if it is." Just a hunch. She squealed, ducking under his arm to squirm away from him and run to her side of the car.

Ma Quirke came out of the house then, her brown-black hair falling down her back in a long ponytail over her red flannel shirt like she'd just stepped out of a painting of farm life. "Don't want you two getting hungry on the way up." Accepting no argument, she opened the back door of the car and set the small quilted carrier and a wide thermos on the seat. Innes couldn't do anything but smile, appreciative of having people who loved him enough to fuss. "Now, it's moose stew leftover from last night, so you'll have to pull over to eat, but you'll probably need a rest stop anyway. There's wild blueberry cobbler in the carrier."

"Ma!" Kahrin protested, giving up her escape and swinging her legs out of the car. "We have food. And there are these new things called restaurants."

"What she means is thank you," he assured Ma. "Don't you?"

Kahrin groaned, evidently trying to convince anyone at all, including herself, that she felt put-upon by her mother. She ran the few feet to her mother and hopped up to ghost a kiss to her cheek. "Your stew is the best."

"I put extra dumplings in the warmer."

That was a win for everyone, in Innes' opinion. He shooed Kahrin with his hands to sheepdog her back into the car. "I want to get there before dark," he reminded her.

"He's scared of the dark, Ma!" Kahrin rolled the window down as he closed the door to finish her taunt, leaning up to make sure there were fewest hinderances possible. "We should get him a nightlight! One of those plug-in ones!"

He rolled his eyes and chuckled with affection. "You're hilarious."

Da Quirke dropped the hood of his car back in place. Innes couldn't say if Kahrin's father had ever worked on an electric car before, but stranger things had happened in the past few days, and Innes decided he was not going to question it. "Everything looks good."

Well, of course it did. The car was only a few months old. He was not going to argue, especially if it wasn't the physical works of the car which were in question. "I appreciate you checking, sir."

"Never thought I'd see such a thing. Electric cars." He shook his head and patted the hood as Innes loaded up. "Drive safe. Call if you get into trouble."

In a matter of minutes, they were on the road, Kahrin having commandeered the radio, and resting her feet on the dash.

"Kahrin."

"What?" How did she manage to look so innocent?

"Oh!" She pointed at her feet. "Does this bother you?" He narrowed his eyes, trying to find the benefit she found in this particular recurring bit they did. "You should have said something."

It wasn't fair, the way she could make him laugh when he wanted to be cross with her. She took her feet down off the dash, one at a time, and stretched with great exaggeration. As if there was a snowball's chance in Ma Quirke's kitchen that he didn't notice the lines and curves of her. "I'm driving."

"And?"

Oh, heaven help him. "I'm just letting you know."

She grinned. "Noted. You're driving. And apparently dead from the neck down."

"I'm sure a resurrection is possible when we get to the cabin." A smile stretched over his face. It felt good, no not just the impending sex stuff, because their friendship had never been about that, but to be getting away. Just the two of them, without having anything or anyone else demanding their time. "Really, I'm just glad we can do this."

"Me too, Pretty Mouth." She grasped his shoulder for a single squeeze, then sat back against the seat, a little too quiet for Innes to believe it would last. "You really don't like

André?"

The speed with which she could change directions, whether running or in conversation. "He's...an ass, Kahrin. He has no right to talk to you like that. To just..." He looked at her, briefly, then back at the road. "You're not mad about that, are you?"

"What? No!" She shook her head. Thanks for small blessings, at least.

"I just... What did you see in that guy?"

She shrugged. "I don't know. He came on to me."

"Lots of people come on to you," he pointed out. Surely that had not escaped her notice. She didn't pay attention to things that didn't directly interest her all the time, but the way people treated her because she was pretty definitely fell in that category.

"This was different."

"Different how?"

"Different like he shouldn't have. I mean, you saw him."

His eyes slid to her and back again.

"You know what I mean. Being a hot guy doesn't exempt you from noticing others of your kind." She wiggled around in her seat, pulling her hoodie off and over her head and tossing it into the back. "He's my professor. Was. Or, will be 'was' as soon as I withdraw." And just when he thought she was done, she added, "I think he might be married, too."

"What?!" It was all he could do not to slam the brakes. She'd not mentioned that part before.

"Well, I mean, he dresses nice to teach but shows up to dates in dumpy clothes. He's in his thirties but was okay with sneaking into my parent's house to fool around." She lifted and dropped her hands onto her knees. "He only took me on dates out of town."

"If you thought he was married, why did you still go out with him?" Kahrin's dating habits, while largely none of his business, made less and less sense with every new person she went through.

"He's not married to me." Oh, of course. "He has no ring. I have no proof, other than his car smells a little like someone melted a box of crayons in it. Do I have to ask every guy who takes me on a date if they're single?"

How was she so calm about that? "It doesn't bother you? At all?"

"Should it? I'm not interested in marrying him, or anyone else. I don't care what someone does when they're not with me." She tilted her head. "I guess it might be nice if he was honest with me, but whatever. It makes them easier to leave."

"Amazing," he chuckled.

"Are you judging me?" There was a hint of teasing in her voice, but only a hint. It was largely a valid question.

"No." Was that true? "Maybe a little? Don't you want someone to commit to you?"

"Not André. Maybe not anyone. Why does this bother you? It's not like you're seeking out foundational and long-term relationships." She held her hands up. "Not a judgment. I mean, obviously not the woman trying to kill us, but what about this Emilia woman? The one who helps you with your rent and car?" Her hands lifted again. "Still not judging, so long as she continues being nice to you."

"Emilia's different. She's not," he paused, still unsure how to explain this arrangement with Emilia, "it's just different." His face burned red. Maybe he was still not ready for this conversation, but that didn't mean his agitation was rational. "Do you mind if we don't talk about her right now."

"Of course." She reached over and squeezed his knee. "I'm sorry." Wow, a whole sorry, just for him. "I mean it, you know. Who you spend your time with is none of my business, just so long as they're good to you." She grinned, leaning as close to him as her seatbelt allowed. "I mean, is it fair to deprive me of punching someone for your honor?"

"You'll meet Emilia," he promised. He'd always meant for them to meet. Now that he'd committed to it, there was no going back, even if he wished to. Which he did not. He wanted to share things that were important to him with his best friend.

His phone buzzed, and Kahrin leaned forward to pick it up from the cup holder. "It's Evangeline." Her mouth pulled into a tight frown.

"Shut it off." He glanced at her. "We don't need it right now."

CHAPTER TWENTY-FOUR

Kahrin

Why *did* she like André?

It was a question which Kahrin herself could not answer, not in any way she thought would satisfy Innes. Especially not after he'd punched the man for being crass in their yard. It also did not fly under her notice that she still referred to it as a matter of present tense. She didn't formerly like André. She still did.

Though not enough that she would continue the affair. If he sought her? Even after yesterday, she couldn't say how she would react. He treated her kind of crappy, and wasn't as charming as he thought he was, but it was that lingering thrill of the taboo which enticed her. She knew he was bad news for her.

She didn't want to worry about André right now. So, she didn't.

She also didn't want to devolve into a fight with Innes. Not here and now, while they were on their way up to the lake. It wasn't just the time alone in the cabin to do or not do whatever they did or did not want to. She liked the hiking trails, and the smell of the evergreens in the brisk air. She liked the hard-packed running trail that wound around the lake. The way it was so dark they could see the stars at night, and so clear in the day that each breath felt like it might blow her apart.

She hard-powered Innes' phone down like he asked. He was right: they had no reason to leave it on right now. Anyone who needed to call him could do so by calling her, and if they couldn't? Well, obviously Evangeline didn't need to talk to him.

They'd pulled over to use the bathroom and eat Ma's stew when she saw the first text from André. An apology that she did not care about, and a promise to make it up to her if she'd let him. That sounded nice in theory, but she returned to her plan to not think of it right now. So, off her phone went, too.

They reached the cabin early in the afternoon. Plenty of light remained so they could unload their gear and get the fire going, but the sun had long passed its zenith and was taking the relative warmth with it. By the time they decided to walk to the small cluster of businesses nearby—not much other than a gas station with a convenience store and a little burger shack that hand-dipped ice cream—twilight was settling in. They walked mostly hand in hand, until said hands were needed to throw big globs of wet snow at one another. The cramped seating of the mostly empty burger shack was satisfactory, since it forced them to sit close as they picked over a basket of onion rings and mugs of hot cider. It was the instant kind that mixed with water, but it was tasty and comforting as they warmed up.

"This feels so grown-up," she said as they banged snow off their boots at the door to the cabin. She gave a good stomp before stepping inside to toe them off. They hung their wet things near the fire.

"Putting snow down my shirt?" He knew very well that was not what she meant, as if he'd not stuffed some of it into her pants, and she stuck her tongue at him. Another testament to said grown-up feeling.

"Coming up here alone." She squatted down near the hearth and peeled her socks off as he stoked the fire and added a log. She draped them over anything close enough to let them dry without catching fire, then took his and did the same. "We used to get excited waiting for my parents to bring us here, and now we can just do it."

"We used to talk about that, didn't we? Coming up here whenever we wanted."

"With our own families." She didn't need to tell him how that had changed, their eyes meeting in the low light of the fire. Oh, perhaps he'd settle down with someone—maybe even Kahrin would find someone to put up with her for a year or two at a time—but neither of them had any hopes beyond that. No secret desires to bring a houseful of children into existence, even if she'd been able. If anyone asked Kahrin, and certainly no one did, she didn't need anything more than what they had, right here, right now. Her best friend, making a choice to spend time with her while she made the same choice to spend time with him.

The cabin was nothing luxurious. It did what it needed to do, providing a place for a few people to exist for short amounts of time. The floors were wood, worn smooth over the years, the walls and ceiling both rough, unfinished beams. Rugs covered common and frequented spaces to keep their feet warm, and the rest of the furniture was built to endure wear and tear. Even the bedding was more functional than attractive, though Kahrin rather liked the rustic look of it all. She padded across the floor, quick steps over the space between rugs, to the main bedroom so she could change for the night.

Innes spoke as he followed her. "We could make a regular thing of this, you know."

She looked up from where she was hanging her jeans over a drying rack. "Of what?"

"Of coming up here, maybe a couple of times a year. Or, I don't know. Just somewhere. You and me, traveling wherever. Just as long as we do it together."

She more than liked that idea, and did a poor job of pretending otherwise, her face bursting into a grin no matter how she tried to feign consideration. Sliding up to sitting on the bed, she finally surrendered to her sub-par acting abilities. "Yes. Anything you want."

"No," he rebuked gently, "anything we both want. That's how this works, right?"

She nodded, as it always had been. "Are you implying that I'd ever not want to?" She crossed her arms, daring him to contest her claim.

She watched him as he traveled about the small room, pulling down the shades and unhooking the drapes as he did. The fire hadn't warmed the bedroom as fully as it had the front room, but it would. Her hands rubbed briskly over her arms as she looked around, distracted enough trying to make out their surroundings that she started when he appeared in front of her, only giving her a moment's notice before he ducked in for a kiss. A quick one, at first, and then another, which she was more prepared for and leaned into.

"I won't ever assume you want anything. Just because you don't say otherwise doesn't mean you still want something. It has to be an active choice." Yes, yes, an active choice. Fine, fine. His mouth followed from the pulse point behind her ear along the line of her neck, and honestly, she'd have agreed to anything with the contrast of the heat of his mouth against her chilly skin. She draped her arms over his shoulders, hooking a foot around each of his thighs to pull him closer. "Even this. Especially this."

She leaned back as he urged her, lifting into whatever kisses he left, her pulse quickening until she hardly noticed the cool air. "I feel safest with you." Which wasn't surprising, given that Innes had been her first of everything. There was no judgment between them, or what they wanted from or with one another.

"Do you trust me?" he asked, his words little more than heavy breaths as she met his eyes. She nodded. One of his hands dropped between them and she heard the jingle of his belt buckle followed by the swoosh of leather leaving the denim loops. "You have to say it, so I know."

"I trust you. With everything." And she always had, since they were very small. Since they caught fireflies in mason jars and punched holes in the lids so they could keep them as lanterns. Since Innes told her they couldn't trap actual fairies because they'd anger them, and no one wanted fairies angry with them. She never once saw a fairy, and now they knew why, but she never doubted for a moment his knowledge on the subject.

"And you know what to say if you want to stop?"
"Vigil."

He caught her in a deep kiss, his hands smoothing up her arms until they met hers. He stretched her arms over her head and she tipped her chin up to allow him to explore her throat with his lips. The motion to wrap the belt around her wrists was so quick she hardly noticed, at least until she realized he'd lashed her to the headboard.

Her eyes went very wide, locking onto his, even in the dark. Her breath caught in her chest, and she tugged at the hold just enough to feel the leather bite into her skin. Not enough to hurt, not really, but just enough to tease at the possibility that it could hurt. To reaffirm to herself that she wanted it to.

"Is this okay?" he asked, gentle and sure even with their heightened breathing. His words were at odds with the rough way he pressed against her, the way his teeth scraped over the shell of her ear. A perfect contrast.

She nodded, then remembered the promise of being verbal. "More than okay," she assured him. "I want this. I want it with you." It was something they'd dabbled in, danced around, and suddenly here it was, the freedom to see it through with no restraints on their time (only her hands). Kahrin had always wondered, idly, at the odd way she enjoyed little pains, like being stretched a little too far and held a little too tight, or the way a love bite made the room a little brighter. They burned through quite a few of those wonders, Innes making all of it feel so safe and, most important to her, normal, before curling together beneath the covers. In a tangle of limbs and evened out breaths and heartbeats, they let sleep come for them.

CHAPTER TWENTY-FIVE

Kahrin

The physics of it all didn't make any sense, but Kahrin woke up tangled with Innes, and somehow they kept all of their limbs. She didn't want to move, as warm as she was, and content as she was with the solid and reassuring thud of his heart against her. Her muscles ached pleasantly, and she woke both sated and starving for more.

Yet in her stomach the gnawing sensation that something was wrong wouldn't let her stay in the warm circle of Innes' arms. It was too quiet in their little cabin. It was too quiet outside their little cabin. Or, she was being theatrical. Which meant investigating.

Careful not to move the blankets too much, not wanting to let in the cold air around them, or wake Innes, she disentangled herself, pressing a kiss to his lovely face in repose. He looked so peaceful, and she wouldn't wake him until she needed to.

Her feet touched on the floor and the cold shot through her, making her rear clench and her breasts prickle. On quick, light steps, trying to keep each foot in contact with the floor for as little time as possible while finding respite on some discarded garment or another, she hopped to the stuffed chair. There she claimed for her own Innes' sweatshirt, which had landed there in their hurry to get skin to skin. Pulling it on did no good, as cold as everything was, and she let a high whimper as the cold fabric brushed over sensitive skin. Innes stirred and she held her breath, waiting to see him settle before she continued. She took a deep breath, bracing for the bold task of pulling on running tights. Cold fabric hugging her legs, she ventured out of the room.

The first thing she noticed as she braided her hair, padding quickly through the cabin to the main room, was the fire out. She could have guessed that, given how cold it was, but it seemed odd. She knew Innes had stoked it up both before they'd gotten too carried away—in fact she'd still been lashed to the bed the first time—and after so this very thing did not happen. Perhaps a blast of wind and snow had blown down the chimney and smothered it. There'd been plenty of wood last night, and now there was none, though that could be attributed to Innes' efforts. Socks and boots on, she opened the door to find she couldn't see anything beyond the small porch.

Thick fog hung over everything. Eerie and heavy, and so dense it seemed to dampen all sound. As she stepped out the door, it scattered out of her way, gauzy fabric being torn apart by her very presence. Testing, she stretched an arm in front of herself and watched it shatter into shreds. This was no natural fog. Which sounded ridiculous. If it was a magic fog, she wouldn't even be able to see it, would she? Wasn't that how it worked? She couldn't see or be seen by magic? If the cold hadn't brought her outside, her curiosity would have. Something was happening.

She turned her head, peeking inside the cabin once more, her eyes moving in the direction of the bedroom. She should go get Innes. Whatever was going on, she shouldn't be doing this herself. Besides, he knew more about this magic stuff than she did. She turned on her toes to go back inside.

"Kahrin?"

She paused mid-step, freezing in place. She knew that voice. This was not good. Not good at all.

"Kahrin? Where are you?"

Shit. She started toward the direction the voice called, pulling the door but not managing to latch it.

"André?" She said it quietly at first, then repeated it, her voice shaking. Hadn't her Da removed the bewitchment? "What are you doing here?"

She hopped down from the porch, her steps already falling as she ventured to the trail that wound around the lake. She couldn't see further than a few steps in front of her, the fog scattering with each footfall and closing again a few paces behind her. It made her progress down the path slow, which rankled but also rattled her. Anything could come at her from any direction, and she wouldn't see it until she was upon it. This was ridiculous; she spun about and backtracked toward the cabin.

"Come on, Kahrin, where are you?" he called out again. "Stop messing around."

She turned toward his voice, finding herself off the trail in a few steps.

"How am I the one messing around?" she demanded, agitation replacing her anxious energy. Where was he? Why was he? "What are you doing here?" she demanded once more.

"What do you mean what am I doing here? I need to talk to you."

Was he kidding her? "I think my question covered it."

She looked from side to side, completely disoriented, no longer certain which way the lake was, or which way the cabin stood. "How did you know we were—"

"We?"

Kahrin stopped walking, her agitation rising into anger. "Yes. We. Me and my best friend. You met Innes yesterday." She turned quickly, waving her arms wildly in front of her, trying to move the fog as quickly as possible. Her patience thin, Kahrin picked a direction and strode forward, the snow crunching under her feet. This was going from bad to worse, and now she didn't know how to get back to Innes. "Where are you?"

"I'm right here. What do you mean you and your best friend? I thought you wanted to meet here! I called you!"

Wait, what? The ground crackled, and Kahrin looked down, realizing she was on the ice of the lake. She stopped walking and looked around her, not sure how many steps she'd taken out on to it, and no way to know which direction led to the shore.

"Kahrin." She startled as hands clasped both of her shoulders. She spun around on her heel and faced André, the fog ripping away from in between them. He looked at her owlishly, with blinking, bloodshot eyes. "What are you doing? I don't think—this ice isn't thick enough for this." City men. He scrubbed a hand over his face.

"When's the last time you slept?" She took a small step back away from him, which he immediately closed.

"I don't know," he admitted. When he laid his hands on her shoulders again, his expression cleared. He looked around. "Where are we?"

"What do you mean? You don't know?" She stepped back again, though this time she kept one of his hands in hers. If he was still bewitched, maybe she could cancel it or something. "We're up at the lake. I came up here with Innes." She shook her head, wondering what in the world was going on.

"Innes?" He pointed behind them, his arm stuck out straight. "The guy who punched me?"

"You kind of deserved it."

"Hell, Kahrin!" He tore a hand through his hair. "What am I even doing here?"

"That's a very good question." She crossed her arms. "What are you doing here?"

His eyes fluttered as he tried to work it out. "Your friend invited me?"

"My friend?" The fact that he phrased it in the form of a question was not reassuring. Something gnawed in her stomach. Something screamed in her head. "Do you know who?"

"The redhead." He shook his head. "She said she was his girlfriend. But..." He scrubbed at his face. "It feels like it was a dream."

"Innes doesn't have a girlfriend." He didn't answer, though Kahrin already knew she was correct. She needed to get to Innes. Now.

André grabbed her arm before she'd taken a full step. "I don't care about him. Or her." He shook his head and turned back toward the shore. The shore! They could see it! "I'm married. Did you know that?"

"You're what?" Sure, she suspected it, but hearing him say it out loud stymied her in pulling free of his grip.

"I have a wife. A wife who isn't hot and cold like a teen girl all the time."

She barked a laugh and set off toward the shore again,

with André following behind. "If your wife is so wonderful, why are you here?"

André stopped walking and the fog swirled around them once more. "I don't know." She believed him, even without the confused look on his face. "I left your farm when your father told me to. I went home to Denise and we fought...she's always yelling about something. But I..." His confusion morphed into bewilderment. Whatever had prompted him to come here, he was afraid of it. "I had to see you."

"Denise?" Kahrin scrubbed at her eyes. Worse than suspecting was knowing her name. Knowing that a real person was on the other side of things, possibly being hurt. That confirmation changed everything, even despite her bluster the day before. "Go home to your wife, André."

"I can't."

"What do you mean?" The fog began to lighten, and Kahrin got a better grasp of her surroundings. She was much farther out onto the lake than she thought she'd been just moments ago. But that wasn't what caught her attention. On the shore of the lake stood Evangeline, hair waving through the air like a bright flame clinging to a torch. Her eyes shone bright like molten bronze, even through the fog. She answered her own question. "Because you're meant to distract me."

Evangeline couldn't use magic to influence Kahrin, and likely she'd worked that out on her own, but she could influence others around her. Others who could keep her out of the way, while she...

Innes.

"I have to go. And so do you." She pushed André in the direction of shore and started walking across the ice behind him, her feet unsteady as the air warmed, despite the cold. Her eyes caught a glimpse of Evangeline once more, pulling up on her pant leg. The dim light of morning glinted off of her...leg? It looked misshapen, like the knee bent the wrong way.

"I warned you to stay out of my way," Kahrin heard Evangeline hiss, her voice taking on a shrill quality that made her shudder. Evangeline's foot—a hoof more than a foot—slammed down on the ice, starting a split that creaked and groaned as it spread quickly toward André and Kahrin, stopping just before it reached her toes.

Kahrin stayed very still, afraid to move lest it push the crack that last few inches.

Evangeline was gone so fast that Kahrin could have imagined her being there at all. If not for the crack in the ice.

"Kahrin. Don't move," André called, stepping toward her. "I'll get you to safety."

"No, André. Stop." She could feel the ice splitting.

"Just for once, don't argue with me."

"Stop!" she shrieked. "I have to—" The ice jolted beneath her feet once more, and Kahrin shuffled her steps backward. She barely made it a few inches when the ice finally gave from under her. She screamed before being pulled under the icy water.

CHAPTER TWENTY-SIX

Innes

Not only was it cold outside the blankets, but the dip in the mattress Kahrin had occupied no longer retained the warmth she left behind. Rolling into it no longer helped, and even the blankets weren't doing their job. Granted, he wasn't in a stitch more than he'd been born in, but getting to his clothes meant sacrificing what scant warmth he possessed.

But! No hero let something so pedestrian as a chill stop him from his duties! If breakfast was to be made (and edible), then he needed to soldier on. Bravely, he threw the blankets aside and braced to put his feet on the floor. The yelp he made was less dignified than the manly adventurers in the stories would ever be caught letting, but no one was here other than Kahrin to witness it. A few quick steps to the chair and his sleep pants were quickly pulled on. Someone had pilfered his sweatshirt, which was a mystery for the ages, he was sure. He was tempted to put on one of Kahrin's for the comical effect alone, but in grave matters of life and death due to hypothermia, he couldn't risk it.

He left the bedroom to find the cabin filled with an odd fog. It didn't make sense, at least not at first, until he noticed the front door open and assumed Kahrin had left it ajar. Hopefully, she'd gone out to get more wood. Before his hand could touch the sturdy door, however, it pulled away from him.

"Innes. Hi."

He blinked, then rubbed his eyes with the heels of his hands. This had to be a dream. What was Evangeline doing here?

Reading his confusion, her lips turned up in a half-smile. "Still groggy, hm?" She reached forward and tapped the tip of his nose again, making the same canned *boop* sound that never sounded quite right. "You were sleeping so peacefully I didn't have the heart to wake you."

Wait, what? He looked around the cabin, his face screwed up. "I don't understand. Where's..." His mind went blank. No, not blank. It wasn't nothing in his memory, but the absence of something. It prickled and tugged but he couldn't bring it up clearly. Whatever had been there was just gone.

"Who?" she asked with a laugh. "It's just us. Remember?" Evangeline twined her fingers with his, that sweet scent of sugar on her skin drawing him in. Her eyes searched his, golden brown and inviting. He must have been tired, just like she said, for her irises appeared to be swirling about, bronze and copper and flecks of fire that were there and then weren't. "You wanted to get away, where no one would bother us."

Her thumb stroked over Yelena's kiss and he twitched away from it. He shook his head as if it might dislodge some of this fog. Like the mist crawling about the room had seeped into his brain, making it hard to think. When he tried to remember why everything felt off, the only thing he found in his thoughts was, well, her.

"Right." Innes rubbed a hand over his face, then over his hair, which was more disheveled than usual. Someone had been playing with it. He distinctly recalled fingers skimming across his scalp, pulling the strands gently. But...he didn't let people touch his hair, usually. His eyes fluttered, his thoughts stymied once more.

Evangeline leaned, pressing a too-warm kiss to his brow. "I suppose I should take a little pride in your fatigue."

His face burned at the gentle teasing, but why? It didn't seem right that he couldn't remember passing the night with her. When had that started? He shivered, turning toward the bedroom, spinning thoughts insisting he go back in there, that he was forgetting something. Someone. Maybe both? "You know, I need to find..." Did it matter? He urgently needed whatever it was, and he started lifting things around the room in hopes of jogging his memory. All he could manage were wisps, little snatches of scent memory that didn't give him enough.

Evangeline followed him, unconcerned with the sluggish way he moved about. He found a pair of jeans draped over a chair which were much too small for him, and when he lifted them up, he knew they weren't hers.

He frowned. "Something's wrong."

"What do you mean?" She moved closer, her steps more pronounced in unevenness, and wound her arms loosely about his waist. He could feel her wrists cross at his back, her hands dangling just above his rear where she patted him playfully. "Other than your hands not being on me? You're right; that's unforgivable." Evangeline brushed the tip of her nose over his stubble, pausing at his ear to let a breathy laugh which tickled the fine hairs there. "You didn't have that problem last night."

Okay. That helped. He remembered something to that effect and smiled. "I'm sorry. I'm being weird." He ran his hands up her arms and wrapped her in an embrace. "A little breakfast and I'll feel better."

She giggled, her fingers drawing up the planes of his torso. "After."

"After?" He laughed. The tightness in his chest eased as he lifted his arms to enable her mischief. He no longer felt cold. In fact, just the opposite. Heat spiked through him with every touch she teased along his sides, his shoulders, and up to his chin.

"After." This time she whispered it, the feeling of her breath on his face leaving him dizzy, like he'd stood up too fast from lying down.

He chuckled, his voice taking on that low burr that he knew she liked so much. No, that wasn't right. Innes disentangled himself from her arms and made for the kitchen. He just needed a moment to think. "Just let me get some water."

"What is wrong with you?" she hissed at his back.

"Huh?" Cup in hand, his other hand still on the handle of the cupboard door from which he'd taken it, he looked at her. "What do you—" He heard a shriek from outside. Near the lake. He set the cup down and moved to look out the window.

He thought he heard Evangeline swear. Rather, the tone was like a curse, but he didn't recognize the words. "It's not our business." She reached for his hand once more.

Someone outside called for help, and some of the fog shook loose from his mind. "No, it's Kahrin." Kahrin! She was here, too. Or, instead? He couldn't remember.

The thought dashed away as Evangeline closed her

mouth over his in a hard kiss. He barely had time to react before her tongue had plunged into his mouth, her hands slid up into his hair. She gripped it tightly in her hands, and any thought other than her sweet smell and the almost sickeningly syrupy taste of her kiss fell from his mind. Whatever had seemed so urgent just a moment ago was replaced with only heated thoughts of need. A surge of lust burned in bright, hot flames, and he gave into it. He had to have her, he had to have her now, and he didn't resist as she pulled him back toward the bedroom.

They didn't make it that far. Evangeline decided the table was long enough to wait, and with a surprising strength that belied her rail-thin arms, she pushed him onto his back across the top. The door to the cabin was open, and the fluttering blue curtains allowed easy view of the kitchen, but he didn't care. He didn't care as she pulled his pajama pants down, or when she straddled him. Even the press of cold metal against his hip didn't seem odd, though distantly, he was aware it should have. He needed to be closer, and curled upward, tightening his stomach so he could get his arms around her slim body once more.

"Enough," she hissed, her hands on his wrists and slamming him back against the table. She curved forward, kissing him hard once more, but this time sensation fled, and he couldn't make his arms and legs move. He heard her draw a breath as their lips parted for only a moment, but the motion violently pulled all the air from his lungs. He couldn't move, couldn't breathe. That certainty that something was wrong started once more, blooming outward from his stomach, but still evading his mind even as panic began to take ahold of him. A conflicting fatigue drew him toward sleep, and his eyes turned up to look into hers, seeing them replaced by golden flame, and her hair rising above her in rippling fire. He tried to gasp a breath but couldn't, tried to yell out for help but had no voice. Evangeline's teeth morphed, her canines elongating. Her face buried in the join of his neck, and he felt a sharp stab as teeth sank into his flesh.

A crash came through the door followed by a rough shout. "Help! Innes, help!"

Evangeline whipped her head up, making a horrifying shriek as a blond man stumbled into the room. The man looked at them, stunned at the sight before him. "Are you kidding me, man? You're supposed to be her best friend."

Best friend? Who?

"You idiot," Evangeline screamed. "All you had to do was distract her!"

Distract her? Now he knew something was wrong. Still lightheaded, Innes focused his mind for all he was worth, and pushed hard against the stiffness of, well, everything, and shoved at Evangeline with all the strength he could gather. Granted, it wasn't much, but it was enough for him to wiggle and kick free and shove her off the far side of the table. He rolled the other way, tripping over his pants caught around his feet. He felt blood spilling down his neck as he tried to pull them up, and stumbled to the coat hooks near the door, digging into the pocket of his parka for...Emilia's handkerchief!

Once his fingers curled around it, everything slammed into focus. Except the stars before his eyes. He pressed the handkerchief against the wound in his neck, unable to believe she'd actually bit him. As he flattened against the wall, he saw her for what she truly was for the first time. Her copper hair had become an inferno, towering off her head. Her legs, one of them definitely bronze, bent backward like a donkey's. He knew what she was, but couldn't quite pull the word from his memory. She flipped the table aside, and threw a chair at André, clearing her path toward Innes as the other man's head bounced off the floor.

Outside, Innes could hear Kahrin shrieking, and pushed from the wall just in time to dodge Evangeline's grasp.

"You're too late to save her." Evangeline's tongue ran over her teeth, cleaning what he recognized to be his blood from them. "I've had a taste and I will have the rest."

She lunged with alarming speed, but Innes dropped to the ground and scrambled away. He stumbled to his feet, tossing another of the chairs behind him, and fled through the door, pulling it closed as if it would buy him any time at all.

He needed every second.

CHAPTER TWENTY-SEVEN

Kahrin

The ice gave way beneath Kahrin, and she was sucked under by the water faster than she could let her scream out. Before Evangeline had stomped on it, the ice had been thick enough for fishing. Kahrin swam upward and caught herself on an intact section, but with her fingers bare and the water just above freezing, she knew she wouldn't last long. André made it to the shore. Somehow, he did so with little more than his shoes soaked.

"André!" she called. She could barely see him through the fog, but if he was careful, he might be able to make it close enough to pull her in. Instead, she heard him stammer, and then his feet retreating. "Where are you going? Don't leave—" Her grip on the ice slipped, and she dipped beneath the water. The shock of the cold as she submerged momentarily disoriented her, but she struggled for the surface again as soon as she figured out which way was up.

André was gone, and she was in the middle of a lake with less and less to hold on to. Her limbs kicked and flailed as she tried to get any traction at all. Every attempt to climb up on the ice resulted in it crushing further.

Far off she heard Innes call to her. "Kahrin?"

Her teeth chattered, hard. "Over here! Help!"

Barefoot and bare chested, Innes staggered to the edge of the lake. "Stay...stay," he trailed off.

"W-where am I going to go?" Her sodden clothes dragged at her, making it more difficult to tread water. She slipped beneath the water's surface and fought to emerge once more. She coughed hard and expelled water.

Innes said, "We have to get out of here." No shit they had to get out of here. She watched as he crept slowly onto the ice. "Evangeline," he repeated her name as he sank down onto his knees. That's when she noticed the spray of red down the front of him, splattering onto the ice.

"W-what happened to you?" He reached out a hand, inching forward and she reached up for it, feeling the ice creak as she did.

He pulled on her as the ice continued cracking at their combined weight. Even from the water she could tell he was weak. He lurched forward, nearly pitching headlong into the water. He caught his balance. Barely.

"Get back," she barked. "Back up on the—" She lost his hand, slipped momentarily under.

"I'm not leaving you." He reached for her hand, skittering back as the ice crumbled, and then inched forward again.

"Go!" Kahrin screamed again.

"No," he snarled. "You promised."

He was right. The night they rescued Yelena, the night she'd plunged the knife into her own abdomen. She'd promised not to do it again. Not unless it was a last resort. He reached out one more time, and Kahrin caught his hand, grasping it tight. He backed up, pulling her, and though she could feel his strength flagging, she kicked and pulled as he did. She heaved herself onto the brittle ice as he pulled them toward the shore. Back, back he fell, and Kahrin wiggled, scrambling forward, finally falling onto him, just off the shore, and close enough to stand.

"You're bleeding." Which he probably knew, on account of all the blood currently coming out of him. Shivering, crying, she grasped the handkerchief and pressed it hard against his neck. "She bit you?"

In an answer she hadn't intended to receive, she heard a chilling shriek from the direction of their cabin. Kahrin looked up, the fog dissipating quickly, and there was Evangeline, just off the cabin porch, eyes and hair aflame. Sure enough, her mouth was stained with streaks of what she could only assume was Innes' blood. Right before her eyes, Evangeline vanished, only to reappear a few feet closer.

"Oh, okay. Sure. She can...teleport or whatever," Kahrin managed through clacking teeth. Wasn't that just wonderful?

"Not-not far," he stammered.

"Far enough." She jumped up, pulling at Innes' arm with her own shaky grip to help him stand. "Innes. Innes come on." He struggled to his feet, the ice along the shore slippery and fragile, making traction awkward and unsteady. He leaned on her, and they ran to solid ground. Or as close to it as two people could while leaning on one another and dripping wet. Their feet skidded and slipped, forcing them to favor balance over speed.

"The keys," he muttered, his light skin already red from the cold bite of the air.

"There's no time." She pulled on his arm, keeping him close. Her arm slipped around his waist as she tried not to get distracted by the warmth of him, which she desperately needed. Chancing a look over her shoulder, she saw Evangeline pop in and out of existence once more, between them and Innes' car. "Where's André?"

"I...I don't know. I don't. He was inside."

So, he was likely dead. Great. Which made her only idea feasible when she spotted his car. His stupid smartcar. Still running, and much closer to them.

They made it to André's stupid smartcar and she pushed Innes into it from the driver's side, urging him over the middle console. He stiffly pulled his legs to the passenger side, one after the other, then she spilled into the driver's seat and yanked the door shut. The seat was instantly soaked beneath her.

Evangeline let out that screech again, suddenly in front of them. Her fingers clawed and scratched over the hood of the car.

"Hold on!" Kahrin yelled, throwing the car into reverse, or so she hoped, since she couldn't feel her fingers. She sped back, leaving Evangeline shrieking in front of them, then shifted it into drive. Sitting on the edge of the seat so she could reach, she stomped her foot hard on the gas just to make sure she actually pushed it. Her feet were long-since numbed. The car plunged forward, ramming into Evangeline. If it hadn't been an absurdly stupid and small car, it might have done more than just piss her off. Whatever she was.

With another angry yell tearing from her throat, Evangeline leapt onto the hood of the car, crunching it under the weight of her leg. A bronze leg. Sure. Why not?

"Kahrin," Innes sputtered. "I know what she is."

"That's outstanding!" For all the good it did them. "You can tell me the story later. We're a little busy." For all she wanted to be funny, she was terrified.

"No, I mean, she's mortal"

Kahrin shrank back against the seat as Evangeline pounded her hands against the windshield. "How much blood did you lose?" She shifted to reverse once more, watching as Evangeline toppled to the ground.

"I mean, she can die." He swallowed. She glanced at him, hating how pale he was, and how the handkerchief was soaked through. "We can kill her."

Why was that always the answer to their problems?

"Okay, but we have to be alive to do that." She spun the car about, fishtailing as much as the roller skate of a car could, and sped off, the tires spinning on the ice before finally getting traction. She drove as fast as she dared, not even really sure which way they'd gone. Everything felt as though it were happening in slow-motion. "We need to go somewhere safe." Where in the world was safe from a fiery, teleporting whatever she was?

"Your parents'."

"No." She shook her head back and forth. "Absolutely not. We're not mixing them up in this."

"They're already involved." His head flopped back against the seat rest and his eyes closed.

"Innes. Innes!" She reached with one hand and shook him, desperate to wake him. "No, no no, stay with me. Please." Her teeth chattered together, and her tears burned her cold skin. "You made me promise. Dammit. Both together, or never, ever." They had to find someplace to go. The farm was now officially too far for Innes to survive the trip. "Innes, I need you to wake up and tell me what to do." Where to go. He was always so calm in these situations, or maybe she just needed to believe that.

The first thing Innes would do would be anything to make sure she was okay. He'd do that first. Because he was good, and he was going to be a doctor, and he loved her. Well, she wasn't going to be a doctor, but she tried to be good, and she loved him right back.

Jerking the wheel hard, she veered off the road and pulled over to the side. She beat at the seatbelt until she realized she'd never put it on, and cast about for anything at all to help. On the floor of the car lay one of André's shirts. Or, maybe it wasn't his. She couldn't say, but it also didn't matter. It was there, and she needed it.

Oh, Innes' neck was a mess. She shook her head, tears stinging her eyes while she pressed the T-shirt to his wound. It would heal. Maybe. She hoped. If she knew how to give stitches...well, she'd probably vomit. Instead, she held the shirt tight to the wound. None of her first aid training taught her what to do when someone bit a hole in your best friend's neck. They had no phone, and she knew they couldn't stay here long. Even she felt drowsy, despite the adrenaline coursing through her. Evangeline would find them.

As if Kahrin's own thoughts had summoned her, there she stood in front of them. Hovered, really. She had wings, actual *wings*, leathery and looking like they were straight out of a horror movie. Evangeline's hair whipped in flames against the backdrop of the snow and grey sky. She crashed on her feet to the ground beside the car, her scream rattling the window, and Kahrin curled her body over Innes', ready for the windshield to shatter. A fist slammed against the passenger window, cracking it, though it held. Before she could think about her reaction, Kahrin was back in the driver's seat, speeding off once more.

CHAPTER TWENTY-EIGHT

Innes

"Innes. *Innes!* Wake up."

Innes' eyes creaked open, though the world shook and spun so that nothing was clear. It took a great effort, but he pulled his thoughts into a line as he clung to this tenuous consciousness. The wound in his neck seared, but now that they were in the car, giving him time to breathe through it, it wasn't that bad. Okay, it was still bad, but he needed to pretend.

"Hey, it's okay, Pretty Mouth. Stay with me." He glanced over, noting the white in Kahrin's knuckles and the way she perched on the very edge of the seat.

"I'll be fine," he assured her. His voice felt rough and he could only hope that was not a lie. He pressed the hanky against his neck until it hurt, which did not take much pressure at all. "It wasn't that much blood." At first, though he was sure he'd lost a fair deal more since. "I was just, um," he swallowed, sure that if he wasn't currently bleeding, he'd feel his face heat, "distracted when it happened."

He could see Kahrin's brow crease, and then smooth when she put the pieces together. "So you two were," she left off, leaving him to fill in the blanks.

"No! I don't think so. Not yet." Not that the

technicalities mattered, all things told. "She's strong."

"Yeah, I'm going to need something bigger than this dumb car to hit her with."

Innes closed his eyes again, trying to think through the haze of shock and blood loss. "I have an idea."

"If it's better than one of us stabbing ourselves, I'm in," Kahrin answered. She shot him a knowing look, and Innes was reminded that he was good to exact that promise from her.

"Do you remember the stream?"

"You mean the one that feeds into the lake?" He made a grunt of confirmation. "Yeah. Of course I do."

"If we can get across it, that might buy us some time." Were he in a better state of being, the confused look Kahrin gave him might have prompted one of his infamous sermons about how recent years had taught them to pay attention to stories. Instead, to save time, he explained. "Spirits, certain monsters, of which I assume she's at least part, fear running water. They won't cross it. Maybe can't cross it."

"Right." That was a big maybe.

"It'll take her time to find a way around it."

"There's nothing up there, Pretty Mouth. Just the stream bed, the ice-fishing shanties, and that place where they," she trailed off and he could see the gears spinning together in her expression. "They store all the split wood up there."

"Yeah."

Kahrin glanced at him, then back to the snowy road, her pretty eyes glassy with tears and scanning their path for any side roads. Her whole body shook. "You want to lure her up there. Do you think it'll work?"

Honestly, he was only guessing at this point. "She's an empousa, and she wants my blood."

"Kinda puts a spin on, uh, wanting to suck you off, huh?"

He laughed, despite how dire this situation was, how scared he was, and how scared he could tell she was. They needed to laugh, at least a little. They'd both survived something traumatic, at least for now. Slow on the uptake, he noticed her speech lagging. "Are you okay?"

"Yeah." Which part of that was more worrying? The monosyllabic response, or the fact that he was positive she was lying.

"Don't play brave."

"Who's playing?" She flipped on the blinker out of habit and turned down the first side road they encountered. He gave her a pointed glare, his eyes narrowing tiredly. "Okay, fine. I'm cold, but I'm hot." He could also tell she was shivering. That seemed right for what he was sure would be hypothermia. Likely she even felt fine with the adrenaline spiking through them both.

The side road hadn't been properly cleared, which slowed them somewhat, especially given they were in a car that was barely designed to run on smooth roads. Innes flopped side to side like he was made of rags as they went over the bumps and dips left by snow, melt, and snow again on gravel.

"There's the bridge," Kahrin pointed out as they were upon it. She stopped just before the road became the paving of the small expanse. "It's a bridge, Innes."

"Yes. Now we cross it."

"But," she fidgeted on the seat, quite the sight to see as she was already wiggled so far forward, "won't she just cross the bridge? And follow us?"

"It's still running water. She won't cross it, at least not here." He hoped. "Or right away." Evangeline was desperate, though, which he was counting on. He was hoping she wanted to finish what she started more than she wanted to think through what she was doing. "But she will."

Taking her hands off the wheel to hug them around herself, she nodded. "It's because Yelena kissed you."

"What?"

"Evangeline." He frowned as she huddled in on herself, wishing he had something to offer her. Except he was in only sleep pants, and not very thick ones, either. "Something about Yelena touching you, leaving that mark on you. It changed you." Her shoulders lifted and dropped, her sodden clothes sticking to her and making her look so small and fragile.

"So...what? It makes my blood magic?"

"I don't know. You're the fairy tale expert here."

He reached over to brush her cheek with his thumb. "You know, you're not exactly uneducated in the subject matter." He'd done his best to instill a strong foundation of such vital knowledge as this. No self-respecting lover of myths and stories and heroic legend would allow his best friend to be otherwise.

A shriek split the air, preceding the violent shaking of the car by only heartbeats. The top of the car dented in from Evangeline's metal foot. She dragged her talon-tipped fingers over the top, again and again, in an attempt to dig through the roof. Kahrin screamed, and they both ducked.

"Kahrin! Go! Go!"

"I can't see," she yelled back.

"It doesn't matter. Just drive!"

"What if we—"

"Just drive, Kahrin!" He reached across the middle and pushed on her knee, encouraging her to slam the gas. They lurched forward, and just as they hit the span of the bridge, the buffeting of Evangeline's wings rocked them and she flew backward off the car, the force sending them crashing against the guardrail.

"No! He's *mine*!" Evangeline yelled after them.

Kahrin sat up in the seat, steering back onto the road. Innes twisted through the pain in his shoulder and neck, turning to see Evangeline run up against the boundary of land and water and back again. Several times, like she was a raptor in a movie testing a fence for weakness.

"She can't have you." Kahrin looked at him, her teeth tugging her lip. "Nobody can have you," she amended, unnecessarily, "but she's not taking you away from me." She turned her eyes back to the road and followed it as it followed the stream.

It took a few minutes to find the area he'd intended. The small equipment shed stood next to cords and cords of wood, stacked in ricks for the various campers to come and pick up. Without being directed, Kahrin pulled the car around behind the wood piles and out of sight but didn't turn it off. No more had they stopped than she curled up on the seat, her arms hugged tight around herself. He reached to turn the heat up to full for her.

"I'm so cold." Her words quavered, wringing his heart. She wasn't going to warm up in her wet clothes.

"We need to get somewhere warm." He let out a hard breath and gestured toward the shed. "Maybe in there?"

"No." He lifted a brow at her harsh response. "What we

need is for all this magic shit to stop coming after us. Wanting to kill us. Wanting us to kill someone else. Wanting to drink our blood!" Her voice rose with every syllable, until he realized she was crying. Sobbing. She heaved in ways he'd not seen in a long time, and it stung.

Leaning his head against the rest once more, he braced. They needed a plan. Steps to follow. If he could get her focused on doing something, she wouldn't fall apart. "André seems like he'd keep an emergency kit. Can you get out and look?"

"Right. Right." He was sure she was wondering what had happened to André. Innes didn't know and didn't offer a guess. He didn't want to lie and suggest he was fine, but he also didn't want to worry her needlessly. She didn't argue, or ask, and simply got out of the car to check for the emergency kit. "It's here. And an overnight bag."

This wasn't the time to think on what André's intentions had been. They needed to just focus on the fact that they had something that would help. Kahrin grabbed the bag from the tiny hatch and helped Innes out of the passenger side. Together, they hobbled inside the shed, which was cramped and full of tools. The only light came from a vent near the roof and was just enough to let them see the outlines of their surroundings. There, in the corner, was a small kerosene heater.

"Come on," he managed as dizziness made him sway on his feet. Even so, he managed a hint of humor to hopefully keep them both calm. "Let's get you naked."

CHAPTER TWENTY-NINE

Kahrin

"Stop covering it up. I can't clean it if you do that." Kahrin pulled the emergency blanket aside and dabbed more iodine on the ugly wound in Innes' neck.

Innes, of course, pulled the blanket back over it, exactly like she'd just told him not to. "When you move the blanket, you let out the body heat." He tightened his arm around her back, pulling her chest to his.

"The cold isn't going to kill me. If you get some weird magical infection—"

"It could," he reminded her.

"Don't interrupt me!" To anyone who wasn't them, it might have sounded like a fight. She supposed it was, in their own way. The back and forth bickering that they fell into as easily as they did laughing. If only anything was funny right now. "Yes, but what if evil girlfriend venom is a thing?"

"She's an empousa." Had Innes been in better shape, she might have been blessed with one of his withering glares. Right now she could really use one of those withering glares. Even a *hm* as he repeated the name of the creature pursuing them. "She—she can fly short distances, teleport in little bursts. She's not my girlfriend," he added unnecessarily.

"I don't think she knows that." Or, maybe he was just a snack. Kahrin had no idea, and really did not want to find out what an empousa did or did not do with people whose blood they wanted.

Innes relented, at least for the moment with a huff, and loosened his arms around her waist enough for her to reach for the first aid kit once more. At least her teeth had stopped chattering, leaving her just shaking. It was enough that his wound was clean and that he'd stopped bleeding. She dressed it, as best she could, though another incident like back at the cabin would undo her work.

"There. It's not pretty, but it'll hold."

"Will I be marred forever?" he asked. Dramatic as always.

"Fortunately for you, I dig scars." She rolled her eyes while pulling the blanket tight about them again, pressing herself close while he hugged her. His skin felt hot against hers, but she didn't mind. Now that she was out of her sodden clothes she felt worlds better, and now that Innes wasn't spurting blood from his neck, she felt calmer. "And I'm sure your someday hapless maiden will as well. It'll make for a great story."

He laughed, soft and weak. Too weak. She tried not to think about the way he'd seemed so listless in the car. André, for all his faults, had a surprisingly thorough survival kit in his stupid smartcar, and now that Innes had a sports drink to sip on, he was doing much better. He was still far too pale, and she was unlikely to relax until she could at least get him to Da. "Thank you," he murmured into the top of her head. "For taking care of me."

"Of course." She leaned back, tipping her face up so she could see his warm brown eyes, barely discernible in the dark. "Of course I take care of you. And you take care of me."

They were both aware they did not have long. Evangeline would find a way around the river, and then she would find them. Kahrin couldn't do anything about it; her immunity to magic didn't counter magical being strength. She suspected Innes' blood was like a beacon for her now.

"We need a plan, Innes," she said. They also needed to move before one or both of them fell asleep. She wasn't the medical student of them, but she did know a thing or two about physical trauma. Also, sleeping when being hunted for your blood just seemed a plain bad idea all around.

Reluctant as she was to leave their warm cocoon, she pried herself away, turning her attention to the overnight bag from André's trunk. Innes had his sleep pants, and little else, and she pulled out a blue button-down and a bright red pullover, holding the two out for him to choose.

"I haven't gotten that far." He staggered to his feet, slowly enough to make Kahrin frown, though she attempted to hide it. He took the buttoned shirt, leaving her to wrap herself up in the sweatshirt.

She hopped across the small shack to the groundskeeper's workbench, pulling on much-too-large pajama pants as she did. There was a simplistic map of the grounds tacked to the wall. After folding the waistband down to try and mitigate the extra length of the legs, she hopped up onto the bench for a closer look, sitting back on her heels.

"There," she said as she pointed. "The trailhead wraps around the spring that feeds the creek."

Dressed and steadier on his feet, Innes moved up behind her. "How far is that from here?" Kahrin looked at him. Surely he didn't expect her to do that kind of math that fast. He answered his own question. "Provided she follows the trailhead—"

The shriek from outside, distant though it was, told them everything they needed to know.

Innes asked, "What do we do now?"

Kahrin had no idea. "We could get back in the car and drive, but where would we go? And to what end? Evangeline is determined to get you, and she'll only follow us." She turned around on the bench and scrubbed at her eyes with the palms of her hands. This was exactly the reason she did not plan things. She could follow plans if she wanted to, but make them? No. "We can't lead her to our families," found or otherwise, "because that will just give her more firepower."

When she looked up, a resolved sternness had taken over Innes' features. "Then we end it here."

Kahrin blinked. "Oh, you're right. I can't believe I didn't think of that." She knew her snark wasn't helping anything. She let her eyes close a moment, then breathed out a hard sigh. "Sorry."

"Don't be." He reached around her to help ease her down from the bench, then grasped her hand and pulled, expecting her to follow. Which she did. "We need a few things." Oh, sure.

He tugged until they were outside, but in the overcast light Kahrin couldn't see anything that screamed helpful. Just piles of split wood, the covered wood splitter, and the stump where the logs were chopped with an axe lodged in the surface. "Innes." She pointed once she had his attention. "I bet that would do the job."

She saw his eyes follow the line of her arm to where

she pointed at the stump and axe. "You want to kill her? With an axe?" She could tell from the way his words poured slowly from that eponymous mouth of his he did not like the idea. She also noticed that he didn't object. "It might work."

Kahrin shrugged. "I know you don't think I pay attention to stories, but I do. I know that taking the head off of something usually stops it, magical or otherwise." Too soon for humor? Maybe.

"Funny how that works," Innes responded drily. Okay, maybe humor was not out of place.

A rush of tingles flew up Kahrin's back as Evangeline's scream sounded once more, this time much closer. Either she was treading the far bank, waiting for them to be dumb enough to try crossing back, or she'd found the trailhead, and with it her way around the spring.

It didn't take long to get their answer. The air warmed quickly as she flew into sight at the bottom of where the ground sloped, her leathery wings giving the heat an Aeolian push in their direction. She didn't fly far, Kahrin noticed. More like she leapt, her wings allowing her to glide a considerable distance each time.

"Help me," she hollered to Innes, pressing both hands flat against the end of a cord of cut wood and shoving her weight against it. It barely rocked, the wood staying in place while the rough bark bit into her palms. Innes leaned his shoulder into it beside her, too weakened to be of much use until Kahrin decided it might fall better if shoved from the side. Both of them leaned into the cut sides. The stacked rows were less stable from this direction and eventually the top wavered and wood toppled over sideways. Evangeline attempted to leap over it, but the tumult carried her back down the incline. It wouldn't give them much, but as the wood piled over Evangeline, it would have to be enough.

They took to heel, and only a few steps later did Kahrin realize that Innes wasn't right beside her. She turned about, bare feet skidding on the cold ground as Innes wrenched at the axe with both hands. He stutter-stepped as it let go of its resting place, and she lurched to help him.

"Go!" he growled between his teeth.

"No." He'd exacted a promise from her, and she'd accept no less from him.

"Dammit, Kahrin." If there was more to follow, it was replaced by the emergent need to defend them as Evangeline freed herself of the piled wood and lunged at him. He swung the axe in a wobbly arc, and, given how much she'd seen him helping Da with cutting wood, Kahrin could tell he was tired.

Evangeline dodged out of the path of the blade. Or so Kahrin thought.

CHAPTER THIRTY

Innes

He hadn't been sure, when he grasped the worn-smooth handle of the axe, wedged into the chipped and marred stump, that he'd be able to pull it out. A moment of Arthurian-inspired hope later and it was free, in his hands. His grip, shaky from lost blood, wasn't giving him any confidence, but there was no time for doubt, either.

Another thing there was no time for was arguing with Kahrin. He'd known before he snarled at her that she'd not go, that streak of stubbornness he loved so much was her greatest enemy as much as it was a boon. Inside he knew that it was only fair, having exacted a promise not to throw herself into danger, that he keep the same, but like all their agreements, it only worked as long as it made sense. It made no sense for her to stay when Evangeline was after him alone.

But like he said, no time.

Evangeline screeched, sulfur tinging the breeze as her eye-catching red hair fluttered in actual flames. He clenched his eyes as he swung the axe, the path of the head wavering. Had it not been for the slight flare of the knob of the handle, it might have slipped from his hands entirely. But the heel of the blade's bit struck her abdomen and sent a shower of sparks before she snapped back with her heavy wings.

"You cut me!" she shouted, her voice shrill and shaking the very air.

"You bit me!" he shot back. That was a thing he should be doing, debating the finer points of what was and was not fair with a woman-turned-monster who was intent on draining his life from him.

Evangeline gripped her hands against the shallow cut. Honestly it didn't seem to have done anything other than piss her off. "A unicorn kissed you!" She spat the words like an accusation. As if he'd conspired with Yelena herself to change him in such a fashion that he did not yet understand. "How did a unicorn find you," she sneered over his shoulder toward Kahrin, "with that?"

At times he didn't believe it himself, but it was not her story to know. Innes stepped back, choking his grip up the throat of the axe handle. It was a good question, and if this had been the time for theorizing or sating academic curiosity, he might have attempted an answer. "What does it matter?" He took another stutter-step back toward Kahrin.

"The blood of a True Believer! Do you have any idea how rare that is? How powerful?" Her eyes, flames flickering from them like water pouring upward, seared into him as she licked the blood from her wound off of her fingers. "It shouldn't happen, but it did, and I will have it!"

She lunged then, and this time Innes stood his ground. A rock sailed over his shoulder hitting Evangeline in the forehead, momentarily stymieing her and causing another cut to bleed down her face. "Back off, hag!" Kahrin yelled.

Evangeline shrieked again, launching herself toward them. Innes attempted to shield Kahrin's body with his own and swing the axe at the same time. He misjudged the momentum, missing Evangeline and taking himself and Kahrin to the ground. Fortunately, neither of them landed on the axe as Evangeline flew over them to the other side, crashing against a small fishing boat loaded with gear.

"You!" She hissed, tripping and backing away as she regained her footing, repulsed by the very proximity of Kahrin to her. "His blood is wasted on you." Her fingers elongated into talons, and she rose from the frozen earth and swiped, catching Kahrin by the arm as the pair of friends skittered out of reach.

Kahrin sucked in a breath, blood blooming through the torn sleeve, but rage instead of fear flashed in her mismatched eyes. Evangeline drew her own breath, and shoved her clawed hands forward as she let it out with a deafening scream that left Innes' ears ringing. Flames shot from...he didn't have time to look. Fire engulfed them, the air warbled and seared with heat as Kahrin wrapped herself around his torso.

The flames vanished. Sucked in on themselves until they were just gone, and the heat they'd caused with them. Kahrin's eyes and mouth hung wide, having no idea what she'd just done, but knowing she'd done something. Both of them were miraculously unscathed.

This served only to enrage Evangeline, and with each harrowing scream her hair flamed higher and her wings beat harder.

Innes helped Kahrin from the ground. As Evangeline circled around and regrouped, they darted past her once more, putting the fishing boat between them, tipping it up to make a shelter to crouch behind. "She can breathe fire?" he whispered harshly.

"Why are you asking me? You're the expert!"

A fair point well made. "If she can breathe fire, I can't get close enough with the axe to," what was the end of that sentence? Was he really going to murder her? Was that what heroes did?

Kahrin's eyes flicked to something, then back to his. He knew that look. She had an idea, and he probably was not going to like it. They crouched under the rim of the boat as another blast of fire launched at them, only to hear the air suck once more and the fire blinker out of existence. Kahrin backed away enough to meet his gaze. "She can't hurt me, but we can hurt her, together." She dashed a chaste kiss to his lips. "You'll know when to attack. Go to her."

Oh, that was reassuring. Not.

Walking in a clumsy crouch, Kahrin's fingers wrapped around the pole of a fishing net. "Kahrin, what?"

"It'll be fine. Trust me?"

His teeth ground together, but what choice did he have? "Of course I do."

"Innes," Evangeline sang out, her voice melliferous and enticing once more, an abrupt change from the glass scratching shrieks. "Why are you fighting me? I've seen your dreams."

"Those weren't real," he called over the edge of the boat. "Nothing about you is real."

He had no idea what Kahrin had planned. There weren't that many things to hide behind, even as small as she was, and Evangeline wouldn't be so foolish to think she'd just leave.

"The way you feel when I'm pressed against you is real." The smell of sulfur wafted away, and that dreamy scent of spun sugar replaced it. His eyes fluttered as he tried to keep his senses, much easier with Kahrin's hand clasped in his. "You're going to die anyway. At least it can be enjoyable."

"You're awfully sure of yourself." He peeked around the stern of the boat at Evangeline. Her wings and talons were gone, her human form intact once more. With only the flips of flame at the ends of her hair to give the truth away, she crept closer on her uneven gait. He felt Kahrin's hand pull away, and with it, the clarity of the situation.

"I'm sure of you," Evangeline hummed. "I do like you. I wish I could keep you for my own."

His head began to spin, and he felt, more than heard, the soft scrape of her fingers against the flat bottom of the boat. "Do you have to kill me? You don't have to take it all at once, do you?" He took a deep breath, steeling himself for meeting her molten eyes, and rose to his feet, stepping around the boat. "I could let you feed whenever you wanted." Past the boat, Kahrin crept around the far side of a cord of wood, and slipped out of sight.

Evangeline smiled, reaching out slowly with one finger, pleased to see she had him under her control once more. She drew him closer with only her crooked knuckle, needing no pressure at all to compel him. "Tempting, but so is the rush from your blood." She tapped his chin. "I don't know if I could stop myself. Or if I want to."

His fingers trembled as she peeled back the tape and gauze Kahrin had used to staunch his wound. Evangeline's tongue slid over the points of her teeth as a dazzling smile turned her lips. He'd forgotten how pretty she was since this morning, when...when...why couldn't he remember this morning? His body slugged along like it was walking underwater of its own accord, fighting against the tide for every step. Her lips were soft against his, and more so as they moved over the line of his jaw, his neck. He felt his fingers loosen on the handle of the axe, struggling to recall why he had it at all. He didn't even flinch at the shooting pain of Evangeline's teeth sinking into the wound once more, at the slight rush from the way she fed. Distantly he thought that there should have been someone else here. But who else could he possibly need, now that he had Evangeline?

The metal of the fishing net made a hollow ring as it connected with Evangeline's head from behind, sending her staggering away, blood-drunk and screaming. Innes gasped in a sharp breath, clutching the end of the shirt he wore in his fist and holding it over the freshly reopened wound. Reality recoiled back into him with abrupt but fuzzy clarity. That had been Kahrin's plan? Some days Kahrin really tested his trust. Now, as always, it was rewarded.

She swung the net again, this time trapping it over Evangeline's head. The mesh began to singe and melt, but the loop of metal slid around her shoulders, trapping her arms. It was then that Kahrin yanked her close. The two women grappled, leaving Innes blinking away the haze as he heard Kahrin shout, "Innes, now!"

Stars swimming in front of his eyes, he snapped out of the stupor of pain and blood loss into action. Kahrin wrapped her arms around Evangeline and they tumbled to the ground. A sudden coolness enveloped them as Evangeline's hair fell into regular, copper locks once more, despite her writhing and fighting against Kahrin. "Innes!" Kahrin screeched once again, this time her voice sharp with pain. Even in her human form, Evangeline was stronger.

BLOOD OF THE TRUE BELIEVER

Still unsteady, Innes remembered the axe in his hand. The pair before him swam in his vision, slipping in and out of focus, the images of them overlapping and merging in a frenzy. He didn't know if he had enough strength or sense to make a clean swing. He closed his eyes, and felt something, and nothing. He gripped the handle, and windmilled his arms in concert with the weight of the axe head hurrying the momentum of his muscles. He aimed for the something, and could only hope the sodden crunch he heard was the right target. He had to trust it was.

Closing his eyes had been a mistake, and the rest of his body seemed to believe that was a sign to just give in to the dizzy exhaustion. His hands left the handle of the axe, and he crumpled to the ground.

CHAPTER THIRTY-ONE

Iskandar

It had taken some work, and no small amount of Grainne's fear-fanned temper, but they'd managed to get both kids into one room. Once he'd been assured his brother was alive and stable, Brodie Cameron was content to leave the matter of watching over Innes while he slept to Iskandar. He wasn't going anywhere. Not this time. No power would move him from this room while they rested, connected to machines that reassured him of the life still in them.

He frowned over the pair, their sleeping forms in hospital beds becoming far too familiar a sight. Color had returned to Innes' face, miraculous with no match to his blood to be found. They'd not even had a chance to make up a good lie as to his odd injuries, though he'd done his best to mask the wound's appearance. There were a good deal of things they'd not had a chance to explain. How long until the world of magic reached out to pull back the reins to ensure its anonymity? He couldn't begin to guess, but it would happen. They would come. They would know what he'd done.

Iskandar leaned against the wall, his spine straight and holding it up as much as it supported him. Arms crossed, he settled into the stillness so many knew him for. He couldn't sit. Even the quiet of the room felt too charged for the ease sitting would bring to him. He watched his youngest child sleep, her hand draped over the side of the stiff mattress of her gated bed as if she'd fallen asleep reaching for the boy's.

Perhaps she had.

He'd been right to place Innes in her path. He was the friend she needed, and then some. Someone steady when she was chaos, as was her nature. He saw a child in need of love, who deserved to be wanted, and the Quirkes had more than enough to go around. They'd accepted Innes into their lives as if he were their own, but none of them had loved him more fiercely than Kahrin. The law of magic said she was never supposed to survive the minutes after her birth. Iskandar always believed he'd spared two lives that night.

Iskandar pushed from the wall and rested his hands on the rail at the end of Innes' bed and watched his breath raise and lower the blanket that covered his chest. Innes was no Adept, but he harbored rare magic. One that could not be snuffed out, or dimmed even by a Hole in the World. He might always be in danger. True Believers always were, straddling the worlds as they did. Iskandar couldn't help but wonder whether he had done Innes any favors by making the choices he did when he interfered with the natural order of things.

His eyes returned to settle upon Kahrin once more, hair a mess of tangles, fanned out over the pillow and her shoulders. He knew when he'd spared her that she would be a stone around his neck, but it was one he carried willingly. He'd not thought through to the way that she would become a stone around the boy's as well, even if he could have foretold his entrance into their lives.

Three quiet steps took him from the foot of one bed to the other, his hands finding the extra pillows Grainne had brought. One of them will want it, she insisted. Maybe so. For now the shredded foam inside it squished in his hands as he gripped it. He watched Kahrin breathe, marveling at how small she looked just now, fragile, as she did when she drew her first breaths all those years ago. She would always be a beacon, a great nothing where something should be. Iskandar Quirke saw the danger a Hole in the World presented. He should have done it then.

Could he do it now?

He stepped between the beds, as if blocking the act from view would protect Innes from the grief that would come from it. This act of brutal kindness. It wouldn't take long. She likely would never feel it or know. He lifted the pillow, poised to press it over her face, and prayed to *Gitchi Manitou* for forgiveness.

His hands released, almost of their own will, the pillow tumbling to the floor. Iskandar dropped his head, shame mixed with a father's love that should never have been allowed to be. He made a strangled sound, swallowing back a sob he could not allow.

Iskandar ducked enough to slide his arms under Kahrin's limp body, supporting her head as he might have when she was an infant, and carefully tucked her into the other bed beside Innes. She curled into the boy's warmth right away, and Iskandar pulled the blankets from her bed to spread over the pair.

He made his choice. It was his choice, and his alone. Iskandar would not allow these two to pay what was his price for it. One day, that debt would come due, of that he was certain, and he would pay it willingly.

CHAPTER THIRTY-TWO

Kahrin

Kahrin's knuckles rapped on the frame of the door to André's classroom. The sound startled him, though he tried to recover. He seemed shaken lately, though he couldn't remember why. "Miss Quirke."

She'd been Miss Quirke for a couple of weeks now. Probably a good thing. Small towns kept no secrets and she heard his wife had left him. Or made him leave. She wasn't sure, but she knew that his car and his clothes being found at the scene of Evangeline's demise when help arrived cast no small amount of suspicion. She didn't know how he'd managed to keep his job. She didn't care.

André looked disheveled in a way she'd not seen him, at any rate. She wondered if he knew there was a singe mark from an iron on the back of his shirt. It wasn't her problem actually; it never had been.

"Hi." She held up her drop form in front of her. "I need your signature for my full withdrawal."

"Oh, of course." He waved her into the room, and she walked slowly, like he was an animal not to be spooked. She wasn't sure how long Evangeline's influence dictated his behaviors. At least since the day he'd come to the farm, but she chose to believe the crappy dates were all him.

He held his hand out for the form long before she

reached the table, and she did the same, handing it over as soon as he was close enough to take it. Not one inch more. He signed it quickly without really reading it and handed it back.

"Thank you," she said more out of habit than actually meaning it. She turned on the ball of her foot and walked for the door, her ponytail swishing back and forth in rhythm with her sure strides.

"Kahrin." She stilled, going rigid before turning to face him once more. She eased herself with a deep breath and maintained her smile. "You're sure about this?"

"You mean moving away?" she asked while not leaving room for him to answer. "Not at all. That's why I know I need to do it." It was and was not true. She knew it was time to move on from this town, but she didn't have the vaguest idea what she'd do next. Luckily she didn't have to figure it out alone.

"That's not what I meant. I meant the other thing."

She didn't give him a chance to explain. She knew what he referred to. Even without the scathing things she'd been called since his wife discovered her part in the dissolution of their marriage, however unwitting, Kahrin knew. "Of that I'm sure." She nodded. Her mouth pulled to the side in a half smile. "I'm too good for you."

Whatever he had to say to that she didn't stick around to find out. She passed the small admin office, dropping her form in the 'IN' basket without breaking stride, and walked out the far doors into the blinding light reflecting off the snow.

"You ready?" The green of the dazzle cleared from her eyes and she saw Innes leaned against the door to the little moving trailer they'd rented. It was a fair bit bigger than she needed for all of her things, but it was the smallest the company had available.

She cocked her head. "You know? I think I've been ready for years."

"I do too." He chucked her on the shoulder lightly.

She looked at the town, sleepy even in the not-so-early morning. "It's weird, leaving. You know, *leaving* leaving."

"How do you mean?" he asked, stepping away from the door and indicating with a tilt of his head she should get in the car.

"We grew up here. It's always been home." She pointed toward the feed and supply store a few blocks down. "I skinned my knee there the day we met you. And over there is where we had our first big fight." And last public one. She'd not forgotten how it had hurt Innes to air their disagreement for all to see.

He chuckled. "Don't forget Mrs. Donaldson's house, where I stole the flower for you for prom."

"She was so mad. It looked pretty though." She lifted and dropped a shoulder. "I still have it. In there, somewhere." She indicated the trailer.

"We didn't just grow up here, you know," he told her, that quiet reassurance in his voice.

She looked up to meet his eyes, noting the silvery scar of Evangeline's bite mark peeking from under the collar of his shirt. He was right. Their families were here, but that was all, and being a hapless part of a world she could not touch would only put them in danger. "We sorta grew up together."

Her smile turned lopsided. "And we'll face the future the same way. Wherever that takes us."

They parted ways behind the trailer and got in on their

respective sides of the car. They both buckled in, but once Innes had pulled them past the city line, Kahrin undid hers and slid across the seat to cuddle into his side.

There wasn't much to say as they made the drive, familiar enough from all her trips back and forth to visit. To find the place where she felt at home, which she knew now could never be a place without Innes. No matter who came in or out of their lives, they would always need one another.

It wasn't until he turned a few streets early that she sat up, curious why they'd taken a different route.

"Where are you going?"

"You'll see." Oh, she'd see, would she? "It's a surprise."

Wonderful. She was great at being patient. Which he very well knew. She wiggled on the seat, doing her best not to barrage him with questions until they pulled up in front of a row of modest little townhouses, each joined in a pair, mirroring one another over the stairs between them.

"What's this?" she asked. An older woman, her grey hair in one of those lovely bobs that looked like they involved no fuss, waited. "Who's that?"

Innes flushed lightly. "That's Emilia."

"That's Emilia?" she echoed, her voice pitching in surprise. "She's not what I was expecting." Though, who knew what she was expecting? Not this woman who had to be at least two decades their senior.

"She's been waiting to meet you."

Emilia swept down the short set of steps from one side of the pair of joined homes, her arms out invitingly as the two of them got out of the car. "My darling man," she crooned, delight obvious in her voice. She fluttered right up to him, brushing a kiss to each cheek. "Terrible of you to keep me waiting so long." She turned, clutching her hands to her chest as her eyes landed on Kahrin. "This must be Kahrin. Are you not every bit as lovely as he promised?" She lowered her voice as she took Kahrin's hands in her own. "He did not do you justice, my girl."

Innes rolled his eyes and smiled. How long would it take him to regret this? Too late now, Kahrin thought.

Not often was Kahrin overwhelmed, but she was now, with such an effusive greeting. She'd wondered if she met the mysterious woman who'd impacted Innes' life so, who'd had a hand in saving it, if she'd be jealous. She expected to be, the way the woman doted on him and whisked him off to fancy events on her arm. Now that they'd met, she couldn't find one shred of it in her heart.

"Now," Emilia clapped her hands together before gesturing to the pair of houses in front of them. "I know it's a little much, but young people need their space, and I cannot bear the thought of you living in those drab little apartments." She tutted at Innes. "Really, I thought you had more taste than that." Wait, what? "Come, come." She pointed to the house on the right. "This one's yours, Innes, and this one," she paused, touching a finger to her full lovely lips in a familiar shade of lipstick Kahrin had seen on the collar of a shirt. "You know, I don't actually remember which is which. A matter for another day!" she announced with a flit of her hands and swept off again in a flurry of silk and perfume.

Kahrin just shook her head, gape-mouthed. "Innes," she started, "I can't accept this."

"It's easier if we go with it right now, while she's excited," he murmured, ducking his head for only her ear. "I promise we'll negotiate the terms later. She wants to help. Trust me?" He shrugged, abashed.

Kahrin tipped on her toes and pecked his cheek. "Always." She pitched her voice for Emilia's benefit and hurried after the woman, Innes quick behind her. "I call the one on the left!"

ACKNOWLEDGMENTS

Wow! Book two! I can't believe it's happened again!

This has been such an exciting journey, seeing my dreams take place right before my eyes. I didn't get here by myself, and there are so many people to thank. Cara, my first reader and biggest cheerleader. Claire, my brutally honest beta reader. Nana, who helped me get this one off the ground. Dominique for absolutely nailing another cover. Victoria, my editor, who is such a joy to work with, who encourages my bawdy humor, and pushes me to be bolder. To Nick and everyone at Atmosphere Press for the guidance, and the wonderful publishing experience.

Finally, to everyone who read, reviewed, and loved *The Hole in the World*. Thank you for loving Kahrin, Innes, and their shenaniganery.

ABOUT ATMOSPHERE PRESS

Atmosphere Press is an independent, full-service publisher for books in genres ranging from nonfiction to fiction to poetry, with a special emphasis on being an author-friendly approach to the challenges of getting a book into the world. Learn more about what we do at atmospherepress.com.

We encourage you to check out some of Atmosphere's latest releases, which are available at Amazon.com and via order from your local bookstore:

Itsuki, a novel by Zach MacDonald
A Surprising Measure of Subliminal Sadness, short stories by Sue Powers
Saint Lazarus Day, short stories by R. Conrad Speer
My Father's Eyes, a novel by Michael Osborne
The Lower Canyons, a novel by John Manuel
Shiftless, a novel by Anthony C. Murphy
The Escapist, a novel by Karahn Washington
Gerbert's Book, a novel by Bob Mustin
Tree One, a novel by Fred Caron
Connie Undone, a novel by Kristine Brown
A Cage Called Freedom, a novel by Paul P.S. Berg
Shining in Infinity, a novel by Charles McIntyre
Buildings Without Murders, a novel by Dan Gutstein

ABOUT THE AUTHOR

Brandann R. Hill-Mann is a Triple Bi (Biracial, Bisexual, Bipolar) speculative fiction author, playwright, podcaster, stage manager, and U.S. Navy Veteran from Sault Sainte Marie, Michigan. Brandann is part of the weekly Bi Bi Bi Podcast, and her short stories have appeared in various publications. She lives in Hawai'i with her family. *Blood of the True Believer* is the follow-up to her first novel, *The Hole in the World*.